BRANCHES AND BONE

THE COLLECTED TALES OF EVELYN HORN
C.R. LANGILLE

Timber Ghost Press

Branches and Bone: The Collected Tales of Evelyn Horn

Copyright © 2023

Published by Timber Ghost Press

Printed in the United States of America

Edited by: Beverly Bernard and C.R. Langille

Cover Art and Design by: Carter Reid

Interior Design: Timber Ghost Press

Print ISBN: 979-8-9883040-1-2

www.TimberGhostPress.com

CONTENTS

1. "Veritas et Tenebris"   1

2. "In Absentia Lucis"   28

3. "Memento Mori"   47

4. Branches and Bone   70

5. Prologue   71

6. Chapter 1   79

7. Chapter 2   89

8. Chapter 3   98

9. Chapter 4   105

10. Chapter 5   112

11. Chapter 6   118

12. Chapter 7   126

13. Chapter 8   132

14. Chapter 9   140

15. Chapter 10   146

16. Chapter 11   151

17. Chapter 12   159

18. Chapter 13   164

19. Chapter 14   170

20. Chapter 15   176

21. Chapter 16   185

22. Epilogue   191

About the Author   193

"Veritas et Tenebris"

U tah Territories, 1862

As the stagecoach entered the town of Fairfield, the setting sun cast a brilliant display of pinks, reds, and oranges across the forest of cedar trees that decorated the mountainside. It hadn't been a long journey from Salt Lake, but Evelyn Horn had already traveled a long way in the last few weeks.

It had rained during her ride over, and the smell of damp earth mixed with sage was heavy in the air. It was a welcome reprieve from the smells of the city, but Evelyn found the vast openness and rugged countryside nerve-wracking. She was most at home in the hustle and bustle of Chicago.

Evelyn collected her bag and made her way over to the Stagecoach Inn. She caught the stares of some of the locals and figured it was probably her appearance. Even though she was dressed in her travel outfit, it was much nicer than the plain clothes of the Fairfield residents. Or perhaps it was her height. Evelyn had been *gifted* with the genes on her father's side of the family, tall folk that had come from

Scotland, which also accounted for her long mane of russet hair.

The jovial sound of a piano spilled out from the nearby saloon and across the dirt walkway. Inside, Evelyn found a stout man with grey whiskers behind the front desk wearing an off-white, button-up shirt with the sleeves rolled to the elbows. He glanced up as Evelyn walked in, and his nose twitched.

As Evelyn neared the man, the sharp odor of whiskey hit her nose. He cast her a dull stare with glassy eyes. Evelyn merely returned the stare, watching his body sway back and forth like a ship caught in the middle of a storm.

After an uncomfortable silence, the man blinked and rubbed his eyes with bruised and swollen knuckles. "Can I help you, ma'am?" His voice was hoarse as if he had been screaming recently.

Evelyn cleared her throat. "Yes. I would like a room, please."

The man fixed her with that blank stare again. His nostrils flared with each breath. "For how long?"

"Hopefully, just a night."

He grunted. Evelyn wasn't sure if it was in approval or dismay. Regardless, he reached under the desk and retrieved a guest ledger. He opened to the appropriate page and slid it in front of her.

"You already missed supper. Breakfast an hour after sun-up. It will be two dollars a night. If you need a hot bath, we can fix you one up for half-a-dollar." He eyed her up and down. "If you are looking for a certain kind of work, you can head over to the Veritas Saloon. They have a flock of soiled doves. You'd fit right in."

Evelyn wanted to reach across the desk and slam the man's head into the wall. Instead, she smiled and played off the rush of blood in her face as a blush instead of pure rage. "Oh, don't you worry your simple head. I'm here for different business."

The man scratched his chin and stared. He let out another one of those mysterious grunts and pointed to the book. "Pay up and sign your name then."

Evelyn signed the book using her alias, Henrietta Carter. As she signed, she spied the other name in the ledger, and her heart skipped a beat when she read *his* name scrawled with hasty handwriting: Raymond Burke.

Evelyn's blood churned. The fool had used his real name.

There was a note in different handwriting next to his signature. It said Room 4. Evelyn glanced up at the keys on the wall and found a key for Room 4. The room was unoccupied at the moment.

The man grabbed the key for Room 2 from the wall behind him.

"Excuse me, Mister?" Evelyn let the word drag.

His eyes sharpened for a moment and he focused on her. "Rook. Gerald Rook."

"Mister Rook. A pleasure, by the way. Do you have a room with a view of these lovely mountains? We don't have mountains like these where I hail from."

He held a key in his hands and then grumbled something under his breath. He grabbed another key off the wall, this time for Room 4, and handed it to Evelyn. Her ploy had paid off.

"Thank you dearly."

"Will you be needing anything else?" The words left Rook's mouth as if they were poison.

"No and thank you. Please do not disturb me, as I am dreadfully tired from my travels. I need rest to regain my strength."

The man wiped his face and spat into a nearby spittoon. "Of course."

Evelyn gathered her belongings and made her way up the wooden stairs. They creaked and moaned under each step, but she was somewhat surprised to see the hotel was in a good state of repair. Most of the buildings in the smaller towns she had visited would fall apart if a strong wind blew through.

She ambled down the hall towards her quarters. As she passed Room 3, there came an odd thunk as if something heavy had fallen inside.

Her curiosity piqued, Evelyn paused to listen, trying to hear if more was going on. A moment later, something slammed into the door from the other side.

Evelyn leaned back out of instinct and bumped into somebody behind her. She whirled around, her hand reaching for the hairpin dagger she used to keep her bun in place. Behind her stood a tall man with a black coat that almost touched the floor, gray hair, and a well-trimmed beard. His dark eyes were warm and kind as he smiled and put his hands up.

"My apologies, ma'am. I didn't mean to cause you a scare." His voice was light, almost melodious.

Evelyn didn't pull the knife. Instead, she put a hand on her chest and leaned into her damsel in distress persona. "Oh my, my heart is aflutter. I do apologize for walking into you like that. I'm afraid I didn't have my faculties about me."

The man lowered his hands and brushed his coat. "No harm done. Please allow me to introduce myself. I am Colonel Arthur Green."

Evelyn had never heard of an Arthur Green in the military. She smiled regardless and held her hand out. "Pleased to meet you Cololnel Green. I am Henrietta Carter. Were you stationed here with Colonel Johnston's men before they deployed back to the East?"

"Oh no, ma'am. I am since retired from the military. It appears they had no use for a cripple." Colonel Green removed the glove from his right hand, revealing a wooden replacement. "I found myself in this lovely town about a month ago, and Johnston's army had long since departed."

Strange carvings covered the wooden hand. They looked like swirls and circles, and some looked like horned skeletons, but he replaced the glove before Evelyn could examine it further. She smiled at him. Smile, that's what her mentor, Miss Warne, had taught her when she joined the Pinkertons. A woman's smile was a deadly weapon.

"It has been a pleasure, but I am afraid I must retire to my quarters," Evelyn said. "I am terribly drained from the journey."

"Of course. Have yourself a good night, ma'am. Perhaps we'll see each other at breakfast?"

"Perhaps."

Evelyn walked to Room 4 and inserted her key. Colonel Green cast her a grin and walked down the hall. There was something about the man that rubbed her wrong. She couldn't quite tell what, but as far as Evelyn was concerned, his story was about as real as his wooden hand.

Once inside her room, Evelyn kicked off her boots and undid her corset. She hated the blasted things, but a disguise was a disguise. She'd catch more attention if she rode into town on a horse wearing pants and toting a pistol.

She dug into her bag and retrieved her Colt Police revolver. She took a few moments to ensure it was in shooting condition. Satisfied, she put it within easy reach on the nightstand and then dug another pistol out of her luggage. This one was smaller and only carried two shots. She could easily conceal it with a leg garter under her dress if she had to go somewhere and look "proper."

Evelyn searched the room. If Raymond had stayed here, he might have left some clues as to his whereabouts. He had come out this way a few months back and kept in contact regularly. His last missive stated he had tracked down his quarry, one Buford O'Henry.

She looked for any loose floorboards, but they were all secured. She searched along the walls, in the desk, around the bedframe, but either Raymond had hidden his cache too well, or there was simply nothing there to find. Evelyn gave up and sat on the bed in defeat. The springs squeaked, yet there was something *off* with the mattress.

She stood and threw the covers off. There didn't seem anything out of the ordinary, but she flipped the mattress over and let out a squeal of triumph. There was an incision in the fabric.

Evelyn reached in and found a wooden box. The box itself was plain and made from pine, about a foot across in each direction, and the thickness of her pistol. She sat on the floor and opened it up.

Inside was a piece of paper, a rolled-up parchment, and an amulet carved out of what appeared to be a piece of jade. The amulet was the size of her palm and depicted a skull with snakes coming out of the eye sockets. She had seen things of similar fashion in museums. However, what unnerved her the most was how warm the amulet itself was. The stone cast a heat warmer than her skin.

The amulet *pulsed* in her hand.

She let out a small gasp, dropping the piece on the floor. Moonlight poured through the window, and the way the shadows splayed across the amulet, it appeared as if the snakes were wriggling.

Evelyn kicked it across the room and into the wall. She stared at it for a few moments, trying to ascertain if it would move, but it either didn't want an audience or her nerves had gotten the best of her earlier.

She turned her attention back to the box, berating herself for acting like a spooked girl listening to yarns about Old Scratch around the campfire. She was a Pinkerton for hell's sakes; she best start acting like one.

Evelyn grabbed the paper and flipped it over. It was a note in Raymond's handwriting.

I am so close to O'Henry, I know it! Madam Vera, who owns the saloon, knows more than she is letting on. However, every time I talk to her, it's the same thing, drabbling on and on about the serpent in the dark or some nonsense. I'm going down there to talk with her again.

Evelyn, if you find this, know I love you and that I tried to get back to you.

-Raymond

Evelyn crumpled the letter and threw it across the room. That fool! Raymond was in too deep and never called for backup. Now he was mostly likely rotting at the bottom of some mining forgotten cave or food for the local pigs.

"God damnit! Why didn't you just let this one go?"

Evelyn knew the answer to that question before it ever left her lips. O'Henry was a wanted man and the bounty was big. However, Raymond wasn't chasing the man down because of some Pinkerton contract. O'Henry had killed Raymond's brother in a nasty gunfight in Kansas. When Raymond found out, he dropped everything and started tracking the dog.

Evelyn should have come with him, but she was already on a detail for the Pinkertons. If she had been here with Raymond, perhaps he'd still be.... She wiped the tears from her eyes and stood. Evelyn would find out where he was, and O'Henry needed to pay for his sins.

The trip had exhausted her, but this couldn't wait. Evelyn grabbed her handbag and placed her pistol in it. She then tucked the smaller weapon in a garter on her leg. Evelyn then took a moment to fix her hair, ensuring the knife was in place. People were stupid, especially with a good-looking lady around, and Evelyn had long since learned how to use that weapon to her advantage.

She headed out of her room and down the hallway. It was dark, with only a couple of lanterns giving out a dull flicker of light. She didn't want to disturb any of the tenants if they were asleep, and she would rather not have folks tracking her movements. Especially Colonel Green. There was something off about that man.

She picked her steps and walked as quietly as she could down the hallway. She paused at Room 3, moving closer to the door to listen, but there was nothing but silence this time. Satisfied that the previous encounter was nothing out of the ordinary, Evelyn moved towards the stairs. She hadn't taken two steps when the door popped open behind her. The lamps went out, bathing the hallway in darkness.

The hairs on Evelyn's neck rose. She turned and dug into her hand purse to find the pistol.

"Hello?" she whispered.

The hinges screamed as the door opened even further, but she couldn't see anything but pitch black.

Evelyn raised her voice slightly. "Do you need help?"

Still no answer. Evelyn took a step forward and peered into the room. Her eyes were quick to adjust to the darkness. The shapes of the bed and dresser stood out, as well as the shadowy silhouette of someone standing in the middle of the room.

There was a whisper so quiet Evelyn barely heard it. She moved closer to the door. Her hand gripped the pistol harder as she slowly started to draw the weapon from her handbag.

Do you seek the truth?

The voice crawled into her head from nowhere and everywhere. She shivered, overcome by the sensation of thousands of spiders crawling over her. Evelyn let out a cry and swatted her body, trying to brush the invisible insects away.

The door slammed shut, leaving her out in the hallway. Evelyn rushed forward and tried to open it, but it was locked tight and wouldn't budge. She pounded against the hard wood with her fist.

"What do you think you're doing?"

Gerald stood in the middle of the hall wearing a deep scowl. His eyes weren't glassy anymore. Instead, they bore a look of anger and bewilderment. He held a lantern in one hand, his knuckles white.

"There's...." She wasn't sure how to proceed. Any iota of the truth would sound insane.

Gerald looked over at the door and raised an eyebrow. He stared at her for a moment. Something burned in his eyes, and Evelyn had the thought that he wanted to bash her brains in with that lantern.

"What is going on out here?" It was Colonel Green's voice.

Evelyn and Gerald turned their attention down the hallway. Colonel Green stepped out of his door. He no longer wore his long coat, but he still had his gloves on.

"This whore was trying to disturb the tenant in Room 3," the man said.

Colonel Green's eyes flashed with anger. "Gerald, that is no way to speak to your guest!"

Gerald opened his mouth to say something but snapped it closed as he thought better of it. He cast his gaze to his feet, face flushing.

"Now Gerald, apologize to the lady."

Gerald kept his eyes downcast and mumbled something.

Colonel Green stepped closer to him. "What was that? Loud enough that we all can hear."

"I said, I'm sorry."

"Sorry for what, Gerald?"

Gerald snapped his head up to Colonel Green. For a moment, that visage of hate found purchase again. However, Colonel Green lifted his wooden hand back as if he were going to take a swing at Gerald, and the big man flinched and shied away.

"Sorry for calling you a whore," he said to Evelyn.

"Good. Now get going. I'm sure some menial tasks need attending."

Gerald sneered at Colonel Green, then at Evelyn. He spat on the ground and shuffled away back down the stairs.

Evelyn wasn't too sure what she had just witnessed, but there was more to Colonel Green than he was letting on. Of that much, she was positive.

"Thank you," Evelyn said. "I, uh, heard something strange in there."

Colonel Green smiled. It wasn't a warm smile in the slightest, more of an annoyed gesture that a fed-up parent would give their offspring just to placate them.

"Oh, yes. That room is quite... interesting. You know, they say it's haunted."

Spooks and specters. Evelyn rolled her eyes. "I highly doubt that. So far, I haven't encountered anything in my life that can't be explained with perfectly normal reasons."

Colonel Green's smile became genuine. "Well, perhaps you just haven't stared into the darkness long enough. They say if you stare into the darkness, you'll find the truth."

Do you seek the truth?

Goosebumps broke out on Evelyn's flesh. She didn't like the tone of his voice. This whole establishment wasn't right, and the quicker Evelyn left, the better. But she had a job to do first.

"I need to get going."

Colonel Green nodded and tipped his hat toward her. "Have a good evening. Stay safe out there."

Evelyn shot Colonel Green one of his own smiles and walked away. As she exited out the front door, she cast a disapproving look towards Gerald. He frowned, wiped the front desk with a dirty rag, and spat another wad of something into the nearby spittoon.

The air outside was warm and dry. Dust covered every-thing, and the wind coming from the west wasn't helping matters. The saloon was close by, and even from the hotel the sounds of people laughing, singing, and enjoying themselves drifted with the breeze.

Evelyn made her way over and pushed her way through the double doors. It was a big place, two stories high. The bar stretched down the length of the wall, and there were several circular tables set up. Men played cards and drank while women who wore almost nothing made the rounds.

An older gentleman with gray hair and a long beard played rousing songs on a finely polished piano. She searched the crowd, looking for the muscle. So far, she had counted four men, two on the main floor and then two upstairs, one of whom had a repeating rifle leaning against the wall.

Her reconnaissance was interrupted when a portly fellow who had an unfortunate amount of sweat pouring from his body saddled up next to her. He pulled her close, and the stink of rotten teeth wafted from his mouth.

"Well now, aren't you a pretty little firecracker? How much for a go?" He slurred his words as he spoke and had trouble keeping his eyes open.

She smiled and slid out from under his arm. "You flatter me, sir, but I'm not that kind of woman."

"What are you talking about? How much?"

He leaned forward for a kiss, and Evelyn spun away. The man lost his balance and fell face-first onto the floor. He let out a groan and rolled over. He hadn't only lost his balance but control of his bladder as well.

Evelyn rolled her eyes and strode to the bar, which was tended by a younger gentleman with a bushy mustache and stone-gray eyes. He wore a brown vest and sported a shaved head.

"What can I get you, ma'am?" His voice was soft, almost sing-song.

"One whiskey please."

"Of course."

He was quick with the bottle, and before Evelyn knew it, a shot of whiskey was in front of her. She downed it and enjoyed the burn as it slid down her throat.

"Another?"

"Please."

He poured her another drink with a sweet smile. "So, what brings you to Fairfield?"

Evelyn drank the whiskey and put the glass back down on the bar. She pulled a handkerchief from her handbag and dabbed at her lips. In another life, she would have preferred to sit at one of the tables and hustle money from the fools here at the bar. But she had neither the time nor luxury to waste at the moment. "I'm in town looking for a friend, Madam Vera."

The bartender's smile faltered. It happened quickly and was back before she knew it. "Oh? You're friends with Madam Vera?"

"Indeed."

The bartender nodded up the stairs. "Up there, last room on the right. She might be occupied though."

Evelyn looked up. The room he indicated was guarded by the goon with the rifle.

She placed a significant amount of money on the bar, paying for her drink and then some. "Thank you."

As she moved through the room, she assessed the bar's patrons. Most folks kept their eyes on their cards, their drinks, or their women. However, a few watched her intently as she made her way towards the stairs. Evelyn kept a mental catalog of those who watched her. They were probably all on the take for whoever ran this saloon, and if things went south, she had to know who was there professionally and who was there just to blow off some steam.

The stairs were well worn by the passing of thousands of boots. They creaked underfoot, but unlike the stairway at the Stagecoach Inn, these gave Evelyn the impression that they could fall out from under her at any moment.

Evelyn rounded the corner and approached the room. The guard leaning against the wall straightened and placed his hand on his holstered pistol.

He stepped in front of her when she got to the door, which was slightly ajar. The overbearing odor of lilac wafted into the hall.

"Who are you and what do you want?" the guard asked.

"I'm here to see Madam Vera."

"What's your business?"

"Please don't be rude to our guest," said a female voice from inside the room. "Let her in."

The man's eyes narrowed, but he moved so Evelyn could get by.

"Thank you," Evelyn said.

The room was dimly lit. Silk cloths of various colors were draped along the walls and the floor was covered in lush carpet. A canopy bed was nestled in the corner and a man was sleeping under a set of satin sheets. He was tied to the bedposts, and Evelyn didn't have to be a genius to ascertain what had been going on earlier.

Madam Vera sat behind a large oak desk. Her ruby red robe fought to cover her assets. She was in the process of tying her long, blonde hair up into a messy bun as Evelyn entered. Just as Raymond's letter had mentioned, she was missing an eye. A purple eyepatch covered the space where the eye should have been. "I don't believe we have met. Please, sit and tell me what brings you to my fine saloon."

As Evelyn moved to the chair opposite of Madam Vera, the guard outside closed the door.

"Yes, thank you." Evelyn had to remember which name she used at the inn. "I am Henrietta Carter. I am looking for a man."

"Aren't we all?"

Evelyn smiled and laughed. "Indeed. This man I already know. He goes by the name Raymond Burke. I believe he came through here not too long ago."

"Tall gentleman with brown hair and a crooked smile, yes?"

Evelyn fought to keep her emotions in check. Madam Vera did know him! "That would be him. I'm afraid he wasn't here to greet me when I arrived. However, I found a missive that mentioned you."

Madam Vera smiled. "Oh, yes. Raymond came over here quite often. Most of the time he was with other girls in my saloon. However, he and I played from time to time."

Words could be weapons. Evelyn's façade faltered, but she was quick to regain composure. There were times that Pinkertons had to play a part, get in deep to get information, but the thought of Raymond coming to this slimy saloon over and over, and especially laying with Madam Vera, stuck in her craw.

"Indeed. Well, do you know where Raymond is?"

Something dripped, hitting a metal pan somewhere in the room. Evelyn looked about but couldn't see anything.

"Of course I do, Sweetie. He's right over there." Madam Vera pointed to the bed.

Evelyn's heart sank. She got up and walked over to the bed. The drip-drip-drip got louder.

Evelyn reached into her handbag and grabbed her pistol, careful not to let Madam Vera see her weapon. She was right next to the bed. The sheet covered the man's face. The DRIP-DRIP-DRIP boomed now that she was next to the man. Evelyn dropped her handbag and reached out for the sheet.

"So, you seek the truth, Sweetie?"

Evelyn hesitated. There was that phrase again. She couldn't tell if Madam Vera's voice was in her head or not. She *needed* to know who was under the sheet.

Evelyn grabbed the sheet and yanked it back. When she saw what was under it, she let out a cry.

Under the sheets was a dead man, pale as a lunger and with a horrified expression forever etched into his face. Blood drained from his open neck into a nearby bedpan.

Drip-drip-drip.

However, it wasn't Raymond.

She whipped around and pointed the gun at Madam Vera, who was now perched on the corner of the desk. She had one leg crossed over the other, revealing dozens of symbols scarred into the alabaster skin of her thighs. Evelyn had seen those symbols before, etched onto Colonel Green's wooden hand.

"You're under arrest for the murder of this poor soul and the disappearance of Raymond Burke!" she said through clenched teeth.

Madam Vera's smile deepened. She put her hands in the air and slid off the desk, moving toward Evelyn like a viper.

"Stop, or I will shoot. I assure you, I am quite the shot with this weapon."

"I don't doubt it, Sweetie. I felt your power and confidence the moment you walked in. Like knows like."

"I'm ain't nothing like you."

"Is that an accent? I bet it slips when you're nervous, or excited, or even when..." Madam Vera raised an eyebrow suggestively.

Evelyn blushed but pulled the hammer back on her gun. "One more step, and I'll blow your other eye out the back of your skull."

Madam Vera stopped. She grabbed her eyepatch.

"Are you ready to see the truth? Are you ready to *know*?"

Do you seek the truth?

Evelyn's face screwed with confusion as Madam Vera peeled the eyepatch back. Darkness billowed from the woman's skull and poured into the room like thick smoke. The smoke slithered across the floor towards her, and the screams of thousands of tortured souls threatened to split her head apart.

Evelyn put her hands up against her ears, but it did little to block out the cries. The darkness swirled around and around, filling the room and blotting out all light until the only thing left was Madam Vera's one eye. It glowed a dark red, burning hot.

Evelyn pointed her gun to shoot, but something grabbed her from behind. She turned and let out a cry of horror. The dead man had slipped one hand free of his restraints and gripped her dress. He leered at her with a rictus grin.

Evelyn screamed and everything went black.

When Evelyn woke, she was face down staring at a wooden floor. She tried to get up, but her hands were tied behind her back. Evelyn rolled to her side. A single candle burned in the small room, and though her perspective was skewed, she knew instantly where she was.

Evelyn was in Room 3.

She rolled to her other side and nearly screamed when she came face-to-face with a wide-eyed man. However, she knew this man. It was Raymond!

He tried to talk but was gagged with a piece of cloth. The large laceration on his forehead was caked with dried blood and his lip was split.

"Raymond, it's okay. I'm going to get us out of here," Evelyn whispered.

With some flexible contortion, she slipped her hands under her feet so that they weren't behind her anymore, although they were still tied with a length of rope that bit into her wrists.

They had taken her handbag and pistol. However, a quick check revealed that the knife holding her hair in place was still there, as well as the pistol tucked away in her leg garter. She reached up and pulled the knife free. Her hair cascaded across her shoulders and onto the ground. She made quick work of Raymond's rope. He removed his gag in short order.

"Jesus, Evelyn, you are a sight for sore eyes," Raymond said.

Evelyn didn't say anything. Instead, she held up her tied hands.

Raymond took the knife and gave her a sheepish grin. "Of course."

Once he got through her bonds, she gave him a strong hug and sank her head into his shoulder.

"I didn't think I would ever see you again!"

"I was starting to have my doubts. I was tracking down O'Henry, and he caught wind I was here. It was over before I knew it. You were right, Eve; I was in over my head."

Of course, she was right, but now wasn't the time to rub it in. If they survived this encounter, there would be plenty of time later, hopefully over several bottles of wine and room service.

She pulled away and gently touched his face. "You look like you've been through a roustabout."

"Yeah, Colonel Green's goon, Gerald. The man's a fool but can hit like an ox."

The sound of heavy boots came pounding down the hallway. Soon the voices of Madam Vera and Colonel Green accompanied the footfalls.

"You got the Pink?" Colonel Green asked.

"Indeed. Feisty one she was. With both of them, we can start the ritual of blood and flesh," Madam Vera said.

One of them was putting the key into the lock from the hallway. Evelyn quickly pulled the gun from her inner thigh and then laid back on the floor, pretending to be passed out. Raymond followed suit.

The door opened and the pair walked in along with another person. Evelyn educated a guess that it was Gerald. Three against two were bad odds, but hopefully, extreme violence would even the score.

"Grab her and prepare her for the sacrifice," Madam Vera said.

"With pleasure." It was Gerald's voice.

A strong hand grabbed Evelyn's shoulder and rolled her over. She planted the small pistol against Gerald's forehead and squeezed the trigger. He had a confused look on his face just before the gun fired and painted the ceiling with his brains.

Gerald fell forward, landing on top of Evelyn. She had to shove him away to take her second and final shot at Madam Vera. The awkwardness of the angle and the weight of the dead body on her threw the shot wide, and the bullet ripped into Madam Vera's shoulder. Vera let out a shriek of pain and rolled into the hallway.

Colonel Green growled and jerked his pistol out of its holster, but Raymond lunged at him with the knife. Green pivoted and fired the gun at Raymond. The bullet hit the floor, sending splinters of wood into the air.

Raymond hit Green, and they tumbled to the ground. He fought to control Green's gun hand with one arm while he tried to stab him through the heart with the other. Evelyn crawled out from under Gerald's body and then leapt to her feet. She threw the spent pistol onto the floor as she ran over to the struggling pair, then she kicked Colonel Green in the face.

He looked up at her with a bloody sneer on his lips and hatred burning in his eyes. They glowed red, much like Madam Vera's one eye had in the saloon.

However, the distraction had cost him. Raymond stuck Evelyn's dagger into his chest. Colonel Green let out a bloody gasp and looked at Raymond, his wide eyes awash with fear.

"You think you can stop us?" Green asked as blood bubbled through his words.

Raymond and Evelyn stayed silent. Raymond pulled the dagger out and slit the Colonel's throat.

Green grabbed at the wound with his wooden hand, and Evelyn swore the fingers twitched when they touched the blood. The man gasped for air as he drowned in his own fluids, then he lay still.

Evelyn grabbed Green's pistol and looked out into the hallway. There was a smear of blood on the wall, and a trail of it leading out to the front. She raced down the hall with Raymond close behind her, busting out the front door to find Madam Vera crawling out into the street. Blood seeped from her wound and stained her clothing, contrasting against her pale skin and blonde hair. She glared at Evelyn with pure rage.

"I have seen your death," Vera said. "You will die in shadow, surrounded by hate. The sky will weep, and the moon will be ripped from the night."

As she spoke, inky darkness slithered from underneath her eyepatch. Her whole body twisted and shuddered. She screamed and the windows of the Stagecoach Inn shattered. The screaming stopped, but a voice spilled out. A male voice.

Do you seek the truth? Shed the lies and embrace the darkness.

Evelyn pointed the pistol at Madam Vera and squeezed the trigger. The pistol barked once, sending a bullet through Vera's good eye. The madam's head snapped back as she fell forward into the dirt.

Evelyn pulled the hammer back and walked towards Madam Vera. She half expected her to jump up and attack, but the woman lay still. Evelyn put another round into her skull for good measure.

The adrenaline rushed from her body, and she began to shake. She stumbled over to the wooden steps of the boardwalk, almost falling as she tried to sit down. Raymond caught her.

"What was that?" she asked.

"I don't know."

The next day, Raymond and Evelyn packed their horses. Raymond had obtained her a beautiful chestnut mare named Oats from the livery. Evelyn placed a metal lockbox into her saddlebag. Inside was the amulet and Colonel Green's wooden hand. Evelyn didn't feel right just leaving them behind. They seemed to vibrate with energy. They would be worth studying, or at the very least locking away from the wrong hands.

She fully intended to stop in Salt Lake to take a hot bath and looked forward to Raymond joining her. But he had that look in his eyes.

She knew that look.

"You're going after him, aren't you?"

Raymond turned away. He had the rolled-up parchment from the pine box in his hand. "I was able to get this from one of O'Henry's men. It's a map to a cave up in the Tintic Mountains just over yonder. He was working with Madam Vera, hired to go collect some sort of shard."

Evelyn pursed her lips. Raymond placed his forehead on hers. "I can't rest until he's brought to justice."

She gave Raymond a hug and a kiss and then mounted her horse.

"Well, lead the way then," she said.

"You can't be serious."

"Dead serious. It's obvious you can't make it out alive without me there to save your behind."

Raymond smiled and hoisted himself onto his horse. "I love you."

"And you're a fool for it. Now let's go! I'll be happy if I never see this town again."

They rode southwest following the mountains, seeking justice.

Seeking the truth.

"In Absentia Lucis"

U tah Territories, 1862

Evelyn Horn stared at the small campfire. The way the embers popped and sent tiny glowing stars floating into the night sky had always mesmerized her. It sent her back to when her father would take Evelyn and her sister, Sylvie, out on camping trips. He would spin yarns about knights in castles going on quests. She never understood why the princesses couldn't just take care of things themselves though. If Evelyn had spent her life waiting for a knight in shining armor, she'd still be fighting for scraps in the streets, or worse.

Evelyn wished her father were here now and that she was merely camping. However, wishes and hopes were about as useful as a golden knife—pretty, but not practical. She brushed a stray strand of red hair from her face and glanced across the fire to her companion, Raymond.

He wore his typical crooked smile, but the way he looked into the flames told her his mind was somewhere else. If she were a betting woman, and she was, she would wager his thoughts were on Buford O'Henry. She couldn't blame him. If someone had shot down her brother in cold blood, it would be difficult to focus on anything else.

Evelyn scooted closer to Raymond to steal some of his warmth and to break him from his reverie. "Do you think we'll find him soon?"

Raymond shrugged. "I think so. If not, we'll have to head back to Fairfield for supplies."

Evelyn shuddered at the thought. The last place she wanted to go was back to that godforsaken town. She could still see the darkness billowing out from the one-eyed brothel madam's skull like some sort of inky snake. And Lord above, that voice...

Do you seek the truth?

She had to play the role of knight and save Raymond from the one-eyed woman and her associate, a deranged colonel with a wooden hand. Instead of relaxing in a nice hotel in the city, Raymond had wasted no time in continuing his search for O'Henry. Evelyn didn't want to see him hurt or dead, so instead of heading back to Chicago, she followed him out into the mountains of Utah. To say she was exhausted would be an understatement.

Raymond had saved her many times before, and if it weren't for him, she would be living a different life completely. He had pulled her from the darkness at a young age, helped set her straight. She loved him, and he loved her. There had been a time, a time before O'Henry, that they were to be wed.

Evelyn pulled her coat tighter around her chest. "Well then, let's hope I am correct. If I am, we should intersect with O'Henry and his gang tomorrow."

Raymond turned that crooked smile toward her and nodded.

The distinct click of a pistol hammer being pulled back sounded from the trees.

"Or maybe you'll find him sooner than that," came a gruff voice.

Evelyn reached for her pistol.

"I wouldn't do that," said another voice, this one from behind her.

Something hard poked the back of her head.

Raymond stood and clenched his fists. "O'Henry, you loathsome piece of—"

A large man stepped from the shadows and smacked Raymond with the butt of his pistol. He was tall and rotund, with a scraggly beard the color of dead pines and eyes the color of the winter sky. His mouth curled into a lunatic grin.

"O'Henry," Evelyn said.

"Ms. Horn, I presume? Heard a pretty little redhead by your name was tailing me."

Raymond groaned and sat upright. He rubbed the back of his head and his hand came away bloody. The man behind Evelyn walked a wide circle until he stood next to O'Henry. He was skinnier with angular features and about ten days' worth of blonde stubble on his chin. He shot Evelyn a gap-toothed smile and licked his lips.

"Ma'am," the man said and tipped his hat.

"This here is Pete the Stick. You already know who I am. Question is, who sent you?" O'Henry's eyes reflected the fire's light and gave him a devilish complexion.

Raymond spat on O'Henry's boot. O'Henry shook his head and raised his pistol back to smack Raymond once again, but Evelyn blurted out, "Pinkertons."

Instead of hitting him again, O'Henry squatted down to look Raymond in the eyes. "See there, she has some manners. A bitch speaks when spoken to. Next time you give me any lip..." O'Henry put the barrel of the gun on Raymond's forehead. "...I'll paint these trees with your brains."

O'Henry grunted as he stood. He walked over to a fallen tree and sat down. He kept his pistol on his lap, and Pete the Stick kept his gun trained on the both of them. O'Henry pulled a pipe from his coat pocket, packed it with some tobacco, and lit it with a burning stick from the fire.

"Well now, Pete, would you look at that? I heard old Pinkerton was hiring girls to do a man's job. Didn't believe it. But lo and behold, we got one of the Pinks right here in our presence. What do you think about that?"

Pete snickered and licked his lips again. Evelyn got the feeling that, left to his own devices, Pete would be doing some unsavory things. She shifted away from him and hugged her chest.

"Are they all as pretty as you?" O'Henry asked.

Evelyn refused to answer.

"Should we deal with them proper, Boss?" Pete asked.

O'Henry took a puff on his pipe and blew a ring of smoke into the air. He scratched at his beard, making a show of the whole process. "No. Bring them with us. I think we can find a use for these two ticks."

O'Henry and Pete disarmed them both. Pete took her Colt Police revolver and stuck it in his belt. He also grabbed Raymond's pistol, and even the little gut-gun she had hidden away in her boot. However, they hadn't taken her bladed hairpin.

Pete used a length of rope and secured their hands first, then tied them together at the waist with about four feet of rope between them. Then, with Pete leading their horses and O'Henry trailing behind, they made their way through the scrub oak and pinyon pines.

Evelyn looked up into the night sky and found the pole star. They were heading north by northwest and higher up into the mountains. O'Henry kept quiet during the journey. He constantly looked over his shoulder and peered into the trees. At one point, Pete started to say something, and O'Henry quickly shushed the man. "You don't want to end up like Bill, do you?"

Whatever had happened to Bill was enough to keep Pete quiet, and Evelyn figured it was best to follow suit. O'Henry didn't seem like a man who was easily rattled, so whatever spooked him in these woods was something to worry about.

They continued up the mountain for about another 45 minutes before coming to a steep game trail. There were four horses hobbled in a nearby glade. O'Henry instructed Pete to do the same to their mounts.

While Pete was busy, O'Henry walked over and lit his pipe again. He kept his voice low. "Probably wondering what's going on, eh? I would be too. But don't you worry your fiery little head about it. You'll find out soon enough."

With that, he wandered over to a large roan in the field and dug some torches out of the saddlebags.

Raymond mumbled something under his breath. She turned to look at him and found he was pale and staring at the ground.

"Raymond, are you okay?" she whispered.

He looked up at her, his eyes unable to focus on any one spot. "What?"

"Are you feeling okay?"

He started to say something but turned to the side and threw up on a lichen-covered rock.

O'Henry shuffled over, looking all around. "You keep quiet now, you hear? Make too much noise and I'll slit your throat and leave you in the woods."

"He's hurt. I think you hit him too hard," Evelyn said. "He needs to see a doc."

O'Henry smiled. "I don't think it's going to be a problem for much longer. Pete! Let's get going."

Pete secured a line of rope to Evelyn and took the lead. O'Henry once again brought up the rear with Raymond in between. They started up the game trail.

The trail was rough, full of roots and loose rock. Many times, the scrub oak made it near impossible to push through. However, Pete appeared to know where he was headed and picked his way through the brush with relative ease. Evelyn could have made it through easier if she hadn't been tied up, but she managed. Raymond was a different story altogether. His legs were wobbly, and he threw up two more times along the way. Evelyn did the best she could to help him.

The trail crested the top of the mountain and ended at the mouth of a cave. Ancient petroglyphs covered the red rocks that stood guard of the entrance. They were similar in style and detail to those Evelyn had seen before, during her travels; however, the subject matter was most strange. The petroglyphs depicted animals moving away from a mountain. Warriors with spears and bows fought a large creature. Having seen petroglyphs before, odd creatures and scary figures weren't that uncommon. However, this one was circular with several wavy lines coming from its body. Inside the creature's body was a star-shaped symbol.

"God damn it, where are they?" O'Henry asked.

"Don't know, Boss. Think they ran off?"

O'Henry took his hat off and scratched his head. "No. Their horses were still down there. Those fools probably went into the cave."

"What is this place?" Evelyn asked.

O'Henry turned on her. The smile was gone from his face. "This is where the darkness speaks. This is where we seek the truth."

Do you seek the truth?

"You best just give up on this, O'Henry, your bosses are dead," Raymond said. His speech was slurred, but he looked like he was feeling a bit better.

"So you killed the one-eyed bitch, eh?" O'Henry replied.

"Yeah, and the fellow with the wooden hand, Col. Green, back in Fairfield."

O'Henry chuckled. "Well, seems like you did us a favor then! Means we don't have to split the treasure down here with those spooky sonsofbitches."

Pete laughed along with O'Henry, and they lit their torches. Pete drew his pistol and entered first. O'Henry had his signature smile on again and motioned for Evelyn and Raymond to go on in by waving his gun at them. "After you."

It was noticeably cooler inside, but not just the regular chill that comes with being underground. This was different. Evelyn's breath formed small clouds in front of her face. The darkness ate the torches' light as well, leaving them with a dim glow. Aside from the chill, there was something else. As if something watched her from the darkness.

"Come on, let's get moving. If those idiots went too far, who knows what might have happened," O'Henry said.

The cave angled down, deep into the earth. They traveled slowly and went through two more torches along the way. At one point, there came a low moan from deeper down in the tunnel, almost like the wind was blowing through the trees. However, there wasn't a wind. The air was stagnant and clammy. It made Evelyn's hairs stand on end.

Up ahead, Pete stopped. "Hey, Boss! You'll wanna see this. I think I found them."

O'Henry grumbled as he pushed his way past Evelyn and Raymond. With both of them distracted, Evelyn reached up and pulled the bladed hairpin from her hair. She put her lips next to Raymond's ear and whispered. "Hold this and don't move."

He nodded. She placed the hairpin in his hands and then began to work her bindings across the bladed edge. It was thick rope and difficult to cut through, especially with Raymond trying to hold it steady while she worked at it in the dark. Finally, they cut her free and the rope slipped loose. Evelyn quickly took the knife from Raymond and began to work on his bindings. She was halfway through when O'Henry came lumbering back up the tunnel.

"Quit your kissing in the dark and get your behinds down here," he said.

Evelyn had to stop. She hid the knife in the palm of her hand and nudged Raymond forward. She kept her wrists together and hoped that O'Henry and Pete wouldn't notice the rope was gone.

As she closed in on O'Henry, an awful stench made her nose wrinkle. It was a smell she'd only experienced a couple of times in her life, and it made her gag. Insides made outside, the scent of blood and fecal matter.

The source of the foul odor became apparent as she rounded the corner. Laying on the floor were the two henchmen O'Henry had been looking for. One's gut was ripped open, and his innards spilled out upon the rocks. Something had torn out his eyes as well. The other was in pieces and strewn about the cavern. Blood covered the walls and floor and even dripped from the ceiling.

"What game are you playing at, O'Henry? Who else is down here?" Raymond asked.

O'Henry turned towards Raymond. "You think this is a game? Far from it. I'm searching for something down here, but it appears something is awake and hungry. That's where you two come into play."

Evelyn blanched. He meant to use them as bait.

O'Henry pushed Raymond and Evelyn in front of him. "Get moving. Pete! Let these two lovebirds take the lead in case we come across anything nasty."

She almost slipped in the gore and had to hold her breath as she made her way through the nightmarish scene. With her back to O'Henry and Pete, she started in on the rope that was tied between her and Raymond. She cut through the final strand and then tugged on Raymond's end to get him to stop.

Pete came walking up behind them and pointed his pistol. "Get moving!"

Evelyn spun around and knocked his arm out of the way. Pete fired, lighting the tunnel up with a bright flash and thunderous boom that rang something horrible in Evelyn's ears, but the shot went wide. She lunged forward and put the knife in Pete's throat. Pete's eyes went wide with shock. He dropped his torch, and he reached up to his neck. Evelyn withdrew the blade and stabbed him two more times in the lungs.

O'Henry drew his pistol, but his boot slipped in the pile of guts. His shot missed.

She grabbed her pistol from Pete's belt with her free hand and shot at O'Henry, using Pete's body as a shield. His body went limp and threw her shot off the mark. The bullet only clipped O'Henry's shoulder. He let out a pained growl and retreated around the corner of the tunnel. Evelyn dropped Pete's dead body and grabbed his gun before returning to Raymond.

"Come on! We got to move!"

Raymond didn't say anything. She turned her attention from O'Henry's direction towards Raymond and found him on the ground. His hands were still bound, but he was doing his best to press against his stomach. Blood soaked through his shirt and jacket and was spreading fast.

"Raymond!"

Evelyn knelt next to him. She quickly cut the rest of his rope and moved his hands so she could see how bad it was. Blood poured from the wound. She had to slow the bleeding. Evelyn pulled a handkerchief from her coat and wadded it up. "Here, press on it with this."

Raymond didn't take it. He looked up at her with a glassy gaze. She knew what Death's mask looked like.

"Damn it! Damn it!" Evelyn muttered. "Raymond, I..." Everything she wanted to say sounded empty.

"Sounds like I got your loverboy!" O'Henry shouted. He peeked around the corner and shot. The bullet hit near Evelyn's head and sprayed her with rocky debris. She screamed and returned fire, but O'Henry had slunk behind cover.

Raymond looked past her. He reached up as if he were grasping for something. "It's dark in here, Eve. So dark."

Evelyn grabbed his hands and pulled them back to his stomach. "You have to keep pressure on this, or you're going to bleed out."

He'd already lost a lot of blood. Even in the dying flame of the torch, she could tell he was pale.

Boots scuffed the stones behind her. She turned and fired another shot, and O'Henry let out a yelp before diving behind the rocks again.

When she looked back to Raymond, his eyes were sharp again and trained on her. "I love you."

Tears welled up in Evelyn's eyes. She wiped them away. "And you're a fool for it."

Raymond smiled. The smile faded from his face, replaced with a relaxed look. A dead man's look.

"Raymond?" Evelyn shook him, but he didn't move.

There was laughter, but it came from deeper down the tunnel. The laughter bounced off the walls and rocks.

Rage boiled deep in Evelyn's guts. She gripped the butt of her pistol until her knuckles hurt. Everything she had done to save him. Everything she had endured to get back to him. All dashed to nothing in a matter of moments. All because of O'Henry!

O'Henry revealed himself from around the corner, but this time, Evelyn was ready. As soon as he appeared, Evelyn squeezed the trigger.

There were no distractions.

There were no impediments.

This time, her bullet flew straight and clipped O'Henry in the face.

He let out a howl and fell to the ground kicking and screaming. Evelyn walked over. Blood gushed from the man's face as he looked up at her with hate-filled eyes. He tried to say something, but it came out as a gurgle, as her shot had destroyed most of his jaw.

The laughter from the tunnel got louder. Whatever it was, was getting closer.

O'Henry stopped his blabbering and peered past Evelyn. He let out a blood-choked sound that could have been a scream. O'Henry reached for his pistol, but Evelyn kicked it down the tunnel. He tried to crawl away, but Evelyn stuck her knife into his thigh. He let out a loud cry and clutched his leg. She ripped the knife out.

"No. You ain't going nowhere." Her accent had slipped through, but she didn't care none. "It appears something's awake and hungry. That's where you come into play." She threw his words back at him.

O'Henry's eyes went wide as the realization sunk in. Evelyn returned to Raymond.

The laughter turned to a giggle then morphed into a wail that was a cross between a cougar howl and a hurt child. It sent shivers through Evelyn's body.

The torch was almost burned out, but through the dim firelight, some of the shadows moved.

The ropey shapes slithered like snakes.

She stuck her pistol in her holster then did her best to drag Raymond back up the tunnel. She spat on O'Henry as she passed, but he didn't notice. He was too busy watching the cave. Waiting for *it* to arrive.

Evelyn dragged Raymond about thirty yards. Her legs burned, and she couldn't find a good grip no matter where she grabbed. Given time, she could get him out; however, time was a luxury she couldn't afford, not with whatever was in the tunnels coming for them. Evelyn let out a frustrated growl and sat on the rock floor. She thought about the night before he had begun his chase after O'Henry. She shouldn't have let him go after the man, should have made him stay with her, but how could she stop him? He promised he would be back soon. Then he wasn't. She couldn't let him go again. It was her time to be the knight and save him one last time.

Not willing to give up, she stood, grabbed him under the arms, and began to drag him further along. After a dozen steps, she tripped on a rock and fell backward.

Back down the tunnel, O'Henry began to wail. In the shadows that danced along the rock wall, Evelyn saw O'Henry trying to fight off... *something*. Evelyn didn't know how to describe it other than a shadowy octopus or a tumbleweed with a ravenous mind of its own.

The inhuman laughter picked up again, and O'Henry's cries of pain echoed through the cave. Then they stopped. The sounds of tearing and snapping took its place.

Evelyn pulled Raymond's dead body up into an embrace. There was no way she could get him out of there and survive.

"I'm so sorry."

"It's okay, Eve. I've seen the truth. It is lovely."

Her heart skipped a beat, and Evelyn dropped him. She scrambled backward until her back hit the rock. He had been dead. She knew it.

"Raymond?"

He sat up. She hadn't been able to bring a torch with her, but some of the light still spilled down the tunnel. Raymond's face was twisted into a large, rictus grin. His eyes, Lord his eyes! They were black pits.

He stood and took a step toward Evelyn, moving like a drunkard who had just stepped off a ship. He extended his hand. "Follow me, and I'll show you the truth."

Evelyn couldn't speak. She shook her head violently. The smile never faltered from Raymond's face, but the eyes grew even darker.

"Shed the lies and embrace the darkness with me. Embrace the truth."

Evelyn finally found the will to stand. She rose and moved away from him. Raymond cocked his to the side and then spun lazily on his heel. He almost skipped down the tunnel, back toward O'Henry, back toward *it*.

Soon the cavern filled with the combined laughter of Raymond and that thing.

Evelyn wasted no time. She turned tail and blindly made her way back up the tunnel. It was slow going without light. Each footstep was exploratory, and she kept her hand along the wall as a guide.

Soon, the sound of something wet slapping across the rocks came from behind her. Then, Raymond's voice. He sang a song, one he used to sing to her when the night was cold and they stared at the stars. But this version was wrong. It was discordant and without mirth.

Beautiful star in heav'n so bright,
Softly falls they silv'ry light,
As thou movest from Earth afar
Star of the evening
Beautiful star

Evelyn moved faster.

Her knees were bloodied, and her fingertips were raw, but she dared not stop. They were gaining on her. Then, from the darkness, was light. Up ahead, the first rays of sunlight pierced the darkness of the cave. Evelyn ran toward the entrance.

"Eve."

She stumbled to a stop and whipped around, gun in hand. Raymond stood there in the dark tunnel, swaying back and forth. He shot her a cold, unforgiving smile. His skin was glasslike, veins bulged, and black under his now thin skin.

Behind him, tendrils of shadow slithered and writhed. A large mass, darker than a coal mine, rose. From within the mass burned a ruby energy, pulsing like a heartbeat.

Star of the evening

Beautiful star

The red star from the petroglyphs. O'Henry's treasure.

Before she knew what she was doing, she took a few steps back down the cave, toward Raymond, and toward *it*.

Raymond opened his mouth and words spilled out. Thousands of voices screamed in unison. Within that cacophony, Evelyn picked out Raymond's voice.

"Come join us, Eve. Come and see the truth."

Evelyn stopped her advance. The thing's tendrils reached for her, moving slow and deliberate. If they touched her, it would all be over. Tears streamed down her face and she aimed her pistol with a shaky hand.

"I'm sorry," she said.

The pistol barked, and the bullet struck Raymond in the head. He stumbled backward but didn't fall. He continued to look at her with those baleful eyes of shadow and smile.

The sun's rays warmed her back and crept further into the cave. As it neared Raymond, the creature wrapped its tendrils around his body before pulling him back into the darkness.

Evelyn found herself at the bottom of the game trail next to the horses. She didn't remember making the hike down or how long she had sat on the cold ground. The sun was high in the sky, and she wondered how it was midday already.

The horses eyed her warily. Evelyn didn't blame them. She was covered in blood, some her own, some not, and she was filthy.

Evelyn took a moment to gather her wits, then she got to work getting the horses ready. She wanted to be as far away from the cave as she could when the light gave way to darkness.

There were things in the dark.

Things that wanted her.

"Memento Mori"

Utah Territories, 1863

Evelyn Horn sat at the bar in a dusty saloon. She had left Manti a week ago, crossing the mountains on her way back east. Evelyn wasn't headed anywhere in particular. She was just trying to keep her mind occupied. She eventually found a town that wasn't on any map, but that didn't mean much out west. Towns came and went like leaves on a tree. It had a saloon. That was all that mattered.

A lock of red hair fell in front of her eyes, and she blew it away, only to have it return almost immediately. She grumbled incoherently and motioned to the bartender for another shot of whiskey.

The bartender raised his eyebrows and gave her a look that was becoming all too familiar these days. It was that disapproving, *are you sure* kind of look. She hardened her stare, which did little, so instead, she pulled out a stack of greenbacks.

The man's judgment never faltered, but he poured the drink. "A bit early isn't it?"

Evelyn looked away. "Not if you haven't gone to sleep."

The bartender ambled to the other side of the bar and began cleaning glasses with a dirty rag. A young cowboy with an expensive, gold-plated pocket watch (in another life, Evelyn would have had that watch by now) and a fancy burgundy vest sat at a table in the corner. It was a stark contrast to her clothes which were wool, heavy, and practical.

His hair was black and slicked back. A soiled dove with dirty blonde hair sat on his lap, doing her best to entertain the young dandy.

Situated near the door was the town's marshal, an older man with a salt-and-pepper beard and balding hair to match. He had shuffled in early in the morning to get a cup of coffee and hadn't left.

Evelyn downed the whiskey. It didn't burn going down anymore. She wasn't sure if that was a good thing or not.

Raymond wouldn't have approved of her newfound habit. Just thinking about him almost brought tears to her eyes. He had died in that damned cave nearly a year ago. Shot by the bastard, Buford O'Henry. Evelyn had once planned to marry Raymond, fool that he was.

Now he was dead.

There was something else in that cave. Something dark, something evil. Something that wanted her.

Whatever it was had used Raymond to try and lure her deeper into the depths. She could still see Raymond's lifeless face, twisted by that dark *thing*.

Shed the lies and embrace the darkness with me. Embrace the truth.

Evelyn shuddered and motioned to the bartender for another shot. Before he could respond, two men in dark coats busted through the doors. They dragged in a young woman behind them, her hands bound with rope and her mouth gagged.

She couldn't have been more than eighteen, with sky blue eyes and strawberry blonde hair. Her dress was disheveled and covered in dirt. One of her eyes was swollen shut.

The marshal stood from his table and put a hand on his gun. "What's the meaning of th—"

One of the men drew a pistol and shot the marshal in the head. He fell back into his chair and toppled to the floor.

The other man sauntered up to the bar. "Two beers."

The bartender wasn't new to the game of death. He poured the drinks and kept his mouth shut.

The man was tall and had a scar that cut up his lip. His face was covered in dark scrubble. Scar looked over at Evelyn and then grabbed his drinks before returning to the table his accomplice had acquired. The man set the drinks down, rolled the dead marshal off the chair, and claimed it as his own.

The man's friend was short and stocky. He wore his brown hair in a greasy ponytail. A red bandana was tied across his forehead, and he had a wild, thick mustache that poked out in every direction. The girl sat between the two, eyes downcast.

The young dandy stood and pushed the working girl from his lap. He produced a billfold from his coat pocket. He grabbed a few bills from within and handed it to her.

"You had better run along now before my associates take an interest in you," the dandy said. He had a British accent. Unlike some of the young men Evelyn had encountered in her lifetime, this man's accent was real.

The soiled dove took the money before disappearing upstairs.

Evelyn weighed her options. Three against one, and who knew if there were more outside. She was a good shot and wasn't afraid of violence, but these odds were against her. She cursed every shot of whiskey she had downed throughout the night.

The young dandy walked over to the two men and the girl and sat down.

The man with the mustache and the bandana began speaking. "We got her boss, just lik—"

The young man raised his hand, silencing his companion. His gaze was locked on the girl's face. He reached out and gently brushed her hair back.

"Did they do this to you?" he asked, his fingers grazing across her swollen eye.

The girl looked away but nodded.

"It's okay, child. Which one?"

"Aww, come on boss. She put up a fight. Damn near bit my ear off!" the mustached man said.

The young dandy didn't turn his attention away from the girl but spoke in a low tone. "One more word, Theodore, and I will hamstring you and leave you in the wilderness for the coyotes."

Theodore stopped talking, his face a shade lighter than it had been moments before.

Evelyn drew her Colt Police revolver from her holster. The bartender caught her eye and shook his head.

"Now, my dear, tell me which one of these ruffians hit you," the young man said.

The girl looked up and glanced over to Theodore.

The young dandy nodded. "Theodore, your hand please."

"Come on, boss, it wasn't nothing."

The young man nodded toward the table. "Your hand. Now. Or I will take more."

Theodore glanced over to his companion, but the other man feigned interest in his beer. Finally, Theodore took off his buckskin glove and rolled up his sleeve. "I'm sorry, boss. I wasn't thinking. You know how I get sometimes!"

The young man nodded. "I know."

In a flash, the young man produced a knife. Evelyn's mind raced on where it had come from, but before she could figure it out, the dandy stabbed the knife down onto the table.

Theodore let out a yell that shook Evelyn's eardrums. He snatched his hand away and blood flew across the room. The knife stuck into the table, and next to it was Theodore's bloody finger.

The girl screamed and burst from her chair, but Scar manhandled her back down.

Evelyn had seen enough. She pushed away from the bar and pointed her gun at the young man. "Let her go."

The young man turned towards her as Scar drew his pistol. Theodore fumbled with his gun but was having trouble drawing the weapon with his new wound.

The dandy smiled. "Gentlemen, allow me to introduce Miss Evelyn Horn. A Pinkerton, if I may add."

Evelyn's mind screamed for an answer. This man knew her, and she had no clue who he was.

"If you know what's good for you, you'll let her go and be on your damned way." To emphasize her suggestion, she pulled the hammer back on her pistol.

The young man smiled. "You're not going to shoot me. Even now I can see the sway in your body, the fight to focus your aim. If you miss, you might hit poor Miss Huntington here."

The girl's eyes were wide, pleading with Evelyn, although she couldn't tell if they were pleading with her to shoot or not. In Evelyn's moment of hesitation, the young man produced another knife.

He was fast. Faster than anyone Evelyn had ever come across. Or perhaps it was the whiskey giving her doubts. One moment he was at the table, and the next he was behind the girl with his knife at her throat.

"Now let us be civilized, Miss Horn. Put the gun down, or the girl dies while you watch."

Evelyn weighed the options. Perhaps her aim was instinctual and her body would take over. Or perhaps she would accidentally send a round through the girl's shoulder. Or maybe she would spend too much time overthinking things and miss the fact that Scar had moved in behind her.

Evelyn spun, but Scar was already there. He caught her wrist and wrenched the weapon away. She reached for her hairpin dagger, but Scar headbutted her in the face.

The room wobbled as loud footsteps that shook the earth thudded up to her. The young man crouched down and lifted her face. "Bring her along. Perhaps two will make *it* happy."

Evelyn's world went dark.

With the darkness came the whispers. It always started as a buzz, like a swarm of flies that had found a rotten corpse bloating in the sun.

However, those whispers began to coalesce into something sensible. Evelyn placed her hands over her ears to block out the noise. She didn't want to hear the words.

The gesture was futile. Raymond's voice burrowed into her mind.

"I'm waiting for you, Eve. We're all waiting for you. Sleeping in the dark. You should join us."

It was Raymond and it wasn't. There was something *off* in his voice. A subtle rage that was unlike the man she had loved. She'd heard that rage before in others. Drunken imbeciles in the saloon, men with a taste for whips and whipping, men who found a knack for teaching via the school of knuckles and blood.

"No," Evelyn said.

"We can wait. But can you? Embrace the truth."

The darkness wrapped itself around her and began to shake violently. She screamed until someone slapped her in the face.

All at once, the whispering ceased, replaced with the crackle of a nearby campfire. The young man crouched down in front of her.

"I apologize for striking you, Miss Horn. However, we can't have that kind of noise," he whispered. "There are things in these woods, things that very much want us dead."

Her cheek stung where he had slapped her. Evelyn opened her jaw wide and there was a pop. Eating would be uncomfortable for the next few days.

"You know me, but I don't know you," she said.

The young man smiled and put a hand to on his chest. "Heavens! How could I be so rude? I am Robert Chamberlain Jr."

He said it like the name was supposed to bear weight, but Evelyn didn't recall ever hearing of a Robert Chamberlain, senior nor junior.

"And what is it we're doing out here, Mr. Chamberlain?"

He smiled. "Well, Ms. Horn, you see, we're about to change the course of history. For too long, the heathens and non-believers have gone about their business without ever knowing the truth of what really exists in this world."

Do you seek the truth?

"So, you're some sort of religious zealot?" Evelyn asked.

"Oh my, no! Don't confuse me with one of those Christian fanatics. I'm not about to dance around and play with snakes. Let them take false comfort with their insignificant god. What I seek to awaken is much older."

Evelyn hoped the man was crazy. However, given what she had witnessed lately, she had a feeling in the pit of her stomach that told her he was serious. She nodded to the girl. "What role does she play?"

"Miss Theresa Huntington? She's a witch, from a long line of witches tracing back to Salem."

Theresa's mouth was gagged. Her eyes went wide, and she shook her head and tried to speak. Chamberlain reached over and removed the gag. "No screaming, or it will go right back on."

"I'm no witch!" Theresa said. "You got it all wrong."

Her voice had a southern drawl that Evelyn was familiar with. Evelyn looked at Theresa and then to Chamberlain. "This little thing, a witch?"

Chamberlain gave her a devilish grin. "Oh indeed, yes. Don't let her pretty face fool you. Underneath that façade is a twisted soul. A soul with the power necessary to awaken the Voracious One. Now, if you'll excuse me, I must prepare."

Chamberlain stood and walked back to his compatriots. Evelyn glanced at the girl. "Don't worry. I'll figure out a way to get us out of here."

She tried to move her hands, but they were bound with rope. Her legs as well. The knots were tight. These cowpokes knew what they were doing. They had taken her gun and her hairpin dagger as well.

Chamberlain sat on a log next to the campfire. He poured some coffee into a tin cup and took a sip. Theodore reached out to grab a wooden ladle but knocked the handle with his cut finger and let out a howl. Scar chuckled from the other side of the fire.

"How many times you gonna do that?" Scar asked.

"Shut yer yap," Theodore said, nursing his injured hand.

"Gentlemen." Chamberlain wasn't looking at his buffoons. His gaze locked onto something beyond in the trees.

Scar drew his gun. Theodore spun in a circle, looking out into the pines that surrounded their camp. A branch snapped in the darkness, followed by a tree falling to the ground.

Theodore fumbled for his pistol. "Shit boys, it's coming! It's gonna kill us!"

Chamberlain stood and crept back toward Theresa. "You can feel it out there, can't you?"

Theresa looked at Chamberlain and then past him to the woods. "You have no idea what's out there."

The fire burned hot, but its light ended at the tree line, unable to pierce the shadows. There was another snap of a branch, closer this time.

What followed chilled Evelyn to the bone. A low wail, almost like a crying woman. The wail grew in intensity until it turned into a gravelly, wet croak.

Theodore ran a hand through his greasy hair. "No, no, no!"

He struggled before he was able to get onto his horse. Scar pointed his pistol at him, but Chamberlain shook his head. "Let him go."

"Boss?"

Chamberlain smiled. "Good luck, Theodore."

Theodore spat and then spurred his horse forward. The horse fought against his command, but Theodore finally got the beast to move. He galloped out of camp and into the darkness.

From the timber came the crack of trees and the rumble of earth. Whatever was out there moved fast.

Two things happened. First, the horse let out a scared whinny. Then, Theodore screamed.

Gunfire echoed through the pines. Four shots, then nothing.

"What was that?" Evelyn asked.

"Some things are better left unnamed, Ms. Horn. To give them names garners their attention." Chamberlain returned to the fire with Scar. "Keep this burning hot through the night.

"Okay, boss."

As the night drew on, Chamberlain read a book while Scar snored loudly. Evelyn couldn't sleep, nor could Theresa. Every time she looked over, the girl's eyes were wide open, scanning the trees and shadows.

"Do you know what's out there?" Evelyn whispered.

Theresa shivered and hugged her chest. Evelyn got the idea that it wasn't from the chill. "That *thing* out there. I can feel it. Its presence is... I don't know how to describe it. You know when it's hot outside? I mean the sort of heat that just drains you and there's nowhere to get away from it. It's like that."

Evelyn looked out into the woods. As if in response, an unkindness of ravens took flight, croaking in displeasure as something disturbed their slumber. Evelyn didn't feel anything crazy out there in the darkness, but then again, she wasn't a witch.

"Is it true?" Evelyn asked.

"That I'm a witch? Does it matter?"

"What does he want with you?"

Theresa shrugged. "What do nasty men want with any woman? To dominate them, I suppose."

Evelyn couldn't disagree. But there was something else. "Your power, what's he plan to do with it?"

"I think he plans to awaken something."

"Can you do it?"

Theresa looked away. "I think so. That's what scares me. When I was young, my power sort of just *manifested*. One day, I was playing out front of the cabin. Ma and Pa were busy chorin'. Well, to say I was bored would be an understatement. So, I needed some friends. Needless to say, I found them. Gave my Pa a huge fright when he came out and found me playing with a bunch of forest critters like they were pet dogs. I think it was the maybe the bear that scared him the most."

Theresa's grin was infectious, and Evelyn couldn't help herself. By all accounts, there was nothing to smile about.

Just as fast as Theresa's smile came, it disappeared. "It scared my Pa something fierce. He got angry with me. Started arguing with Ma about bloodlines or some such nonsense. He never looked at me the same again. He thought he could beat the devil out of me." Theresa turned her head and wiped her cheeks. "This stupid *gift*, as my Ma called it, ain't been nothing but trouble. So I keep it buried deep."

"Well, let's make sure this bastard can't do whatever he plans to do," Evelyn said.

Evelyn was able to untie the girl, taking care that Chamberlain's attention was elsewhere. Once Theresa was untied, she helped undo the knots in Evelyn's bonds. Before they moved to leave, a raven landed on a nearby rock. It cocked its head to the side, staring at Evelyn and Theresa with a curiosity only known to animals.

Theresa smiled and held out her arm. The raven immediately flew over to her. Theresa stroked the bird's head.

"My mama used to tell me that ravens and crows helped usher the spirits of the dead to the other side. If that's true, maybe this one has Theodore's soul." Theresa said. "She told me she had the power to rip my Pa's soul from that bird before it flew away, but she was more than happy to see that bastard burn in hell." Theresa ushered the raven back into the night sky.

Evelyn made her way over to the horses. Her chestnut mare, Oats, was with the others. Evelyn snuck over to Oats and patted her head. Oats shook her mane and nipped at Evelyn's ear.

"I know, I let those horrible people mess with you. I'm sorry," she whispered.

Evelyn dug through her saddlebags looking for her gun, but it wasn't there.

"Looking for these I presume?"

She spun around and found Chamberlain. He held Evelyn's gun belt in one hand. In the other, he spun her hairpin dagger effortlessly.

With a flick of his wrist, he sent the dagger flying through the air towards Evelyn. She turned away, but it still caught her in the shoulder. She cried out and fell to the ground as the blade bit into her flesh.

Theresa screamed and ran at Chamberlain, but Scar grabbed the girl before she could make it far.

Chamberlain smiled and dropped Evelyn's gun belt to the ground. He drew a knife from his coat and twirled the blade on his fingertip.

"Ms. Horn, you are quickly becoming more trouble than you're worth." Chamberlain nodded to Scar.

Scar threw Theresa to the ground and strode toward Evelyn. He drew his pistol as he walked.

Evelyn crab-walked backward to try and create some distance. Scar closed in quickly. Evelyn let out a shrill whistle.

Oats neighed and kicked, catching Scar in the chest. He let out a deep *oomph* as he sailed through the air.

Evelyn scrambled to her feet. Her shoulder blazed with pain as the knife shifted. She gritted her teeth and yanked it free.

Chamberlain rushed her. He was fast, and she was wounded, but her body ran on instinct. Evelyn shifted her weight and pivoted. A half-second slower and Chamberlain would have driven his knife into her heart.

She didn't have time to think as Chamberlain continued his assault with a series of stabs and slashes, all designed to kill.

Evelyn danced back, twisting and dodging. The last one went for her eye, and although she ducked away, the blade still kissed her cheek.

Blood ran down her face and into her mouth. She spat it away, never taking her eyes off Chamberlain. He was a viper ready to strike.

Scar groaned and rolled to his side. Evelyn cursed her luck.

Chamberlain shot her a devilish grin. "It seems your time has come to—"

The telltale click of a pistol hammer locking into place cut him off. Theresa stood behind Chamberlain, Evelyn's gun in her hands. She shook harder than the leaves on an aspen in a hard breeze.

Chamberlain's visage hardened as his lips curled into a sneer. "Now child, put that down before you hurt yourself."

Theresa's eyes burned with hate. That rage spoke a language that few understood but Evelyn was intimate with.

Theresa took a step forward. "You killed my ma."

Chamberlain pivoted so he could keep Evelyn and Theresa in his sights. His eyes flicked behind Theresa. Scar was on his feet and moving towards the girl.

"Look out!" Evelyn yelled.

Theresa turned and screamed. Chamberlain took advantage of the girl's distraction and rushed her. Theresa turned back toward him, and the gun barked in her hand just as Scar barreled into her. The round went wild but clipped Chamberlain in the leg. He grunted and dropped to the ground.

Theresa was on her back with Scar on top of her. She tried to shoot him, but he knocked the weapon away.

Evelyn raced towards the pair, but Chamberlain grabbed her by the foot, and she fell to the ground.

She kicked back and caught Chamberlain in the face. He let go with a growl. Scar had Theresa's arms restrained with one hand and reared his fist back to punch her. Evelyn flung the dagger at Scar and caught him in the arm. He yelled and spun around.

"You'll pay for that," he said.

Evelyn got to her feet, backing away from Chamberlain. "Let that girl go."

Scar smiled through the pain. "Or what, you'll kill me?"

"I'm going to kill you regardless, you lump of cow shit."

Scar laughed. He grimaced as he yanked the dagger from his arm and threw it away. "That's a cute little sticker you got there. I'm sure you'll appreciate this."

Scar drew a Bowie knife from his belt.

Evelyn was wounded, weaponless, and facing an opponent who had a knife and was almost twice her size. However, at least he wasn't focused on Theresa anymore.

Scar ambled toward her holding the Bowie knife in a downward grip. He gave her a grin that promised horrible things.

The campfire went out as if someone had doused it. The woods fell silent. Scar stopped his advance and stared at something behind Evelyn.

She turned.

Standing in the meadow was Theodore. His eyes were milky white, and he cried tears of blood. He opened his mouth as if he were about to say something, but the sound that came from him was like a wailing cat mixed with a bullfrog.

His movements were jerky, as if he didn't know how his legs were supposed to work. Extending from his head was a tendril of darkness, pocked with burning dots that resembled stars in the night sky. Evelyn followed the tendril back to the trees and found its source. She instantly wished she hadn't, as her mind splintered under the strain of what she saw.

Crouched in a large branch was a massive shadow with eyes that glowed with azure hate. It hopped down onto the ground and stood. The thing was easily over ten feet tall. Its body was thin, emaciated, and coated with black fur. Covering its head and face was the skull of a large elk, its antlers stark white against the creature's dusky body. The tendril that connected to Theodore came from the creature's back.

Scar made a move for the horses and snapped a twig. The creature's head lolled to the side, and another tendril sprouted from its back with a wet popping noise. It sped through the air and speared Scar through the mouth.

He dropped to his knees and tried to fight against the tendril, but soon his body went limp. Scar's eyes turned white like Theodore's. He convulsed as the tendril began to pump something dark into him.

The creature stared at Evelyn as it strode from the trees toward her. It lifted the two men with ease and placed them at its side like they were pets.

The thing crouched down so it was eye level with Evelyn. Rancid breath rasped from under its skull helmet. Evelyn was afraid if she moved, she'd end up like Chamberlain's lapdogs. The thing cupped her chin with a skeletal hand. Theodore and Scar reached out in unison, mimicking the creature's movements.

It pulled her closer. Evelyn's instincts kicked in, and she tried to break its arm, aiming for the joint like she had been taught. Evelyn would have had better luck trying to snap a fencepost.

If the creature even registered her attack, it didn't let on. Its eyes bore into her. They were swirling galaxies, the centers of which were massive stars that burned black and cold. It spoke to her, drilling into her mind with the precision of a monkey using a stick to dig termites from a mound.

The words were foreign, their sound making her vomit. Theodore and Scar's mouths moved, teeth clattering as they tried to mimic the creature's tongue.

From their mouths came the whispers of a legion of sleeping beings. Entities waiting for the universe to align in such a way that they could awaken and spread their truth through the cosmos. They slept in the dark caves of a blasted planet, deep down where the suns of a million galaxies could never touch. As one, they stirred.

Yet, the stars were not right, so still they slept.

A tendril wrapped itself around her throat before forcing its way into her mouth. She tried to scream but couldn't make a sound.

The chattering of the two outlaws grew louder, and somewhere deep down in her primal brain she wanted to join their chittering. Then, from behind her, Theresa's voice cracked through, driving the noise away.

"Back to the darkness I command thee, leave this place, turn and flee!"

Over and over, Theresa said the words. Each time, her voice boomed louder.

The creature hissed. It dropped Scar and Theodore to the ground. Everything went dark as Evelyn's eyesight began to blur. Soon, there was nothing but the wet hiss of the monster and Theresa's voice.

Then, there was nothing.

Evelyn floated in a dark place. Her stomach lurched as if she were falling. Before she could scream, she was swooped up into the air. Faster than she thought possible, the darkness melted away and the trees of the forest sped by underneath.

She had the sensation that she was flying. In the distance, a large mountain loomed that seethed with hate and dark energy. It seemed to pull her closer.

Evelyn fought against the pull, but it was useless. Near the top of the mountain was a figure silhouetted by a large bonfire that stood at the entrance of a massive cave. It cast an inhuman shadow that moved of its own accord.

Evelyn awoke screaming and in pain. She was on her back with Theresa crouched next to her.

Evelyn's stomach turned. She rolled to her side, spewing out a brackish liquid the color of mud. Her throat was raw and it hurt to breathe, but she somehow found words. "What happened?"

"I drove it off," Theresa said.

"How?"

Theresa shrugged.

Evelyn nodded. For a while, she lay on her back, staring up at the sky. The clouds shifted, offering her a view of the stars, and deep down in her gut she couldn't help but think about the vast army of... *things* that were waiting to awaken and destroy everything.

Evelyn knew the truth. She didn't seek it, but it found her, and it would haunt her until she died, and perhaps even after.

Evelyn turned her head and looked at Theresa. "So, you're a witch, eh?"

"I told you so."

"Thanks for saving me. Without you, I think I would have died."

Theresa hugged her legs to her chest. "You did die."

Evelyn's heart skipped a beat. "What?"

"The thing killed you. But I was able to bring you back."

Evelyn propped herself up on her elbow. A lock of hair fell into her face, and instead of being red, it was whiter than snow. It was just a strip as far as she could tell, but her hair wasn't what bothered her. It was what Theresa was trying to tell her.

"You have to be joking."

Theresa's eyes went cold. "Death is no joke." The girl handed Evelyn a feather. It was a raven's feather, but instead of being pure black, there was a strip of white.

Chamberlain had slipped away to live another day, although he was now on Evelyn's shortlist of outlaws to find.

Evelyn and Theresa rode out. During the day, the forest wasn't threatening. They followed a game trail that led them to another small town. Evelyn was elated; however, that elation melted away. Behind the town was a large mountain. Evelyn knew this mountain. It was the same one she had seen when she had died. She knew that at the top, there'd be a cave, and in that cave, there'd be answers.

There'd be the truth.

BRANCHES

&

BONE

PROLOGUE

Utah Territory, 1883

Rex Martin didn't know it yet, but he had woken up for the last time in his life. After gathering his gear, he hiked up a small rise surrounded by tall lodgepole pines and the occasional aspen. It was a cool afternoon, though he was hot and sweaty by the time he got to the top. The mountains they harvested the lumber from were high in elevation, and the air was thinner. It made simple tasks like walking up a hill much harder to do. While he had lived in the Utah Territory for the last few years, he still wasn't used to the elevation.

By the time he crested the hill, he was breathing like he had just been in a gunfight. Up ahead, there was a break in the trees. Rex decided it was an excellent time to take a break, plus he could eat the hard roll he'd stolen from the camp kitchen before heading out to find trees to cut down.

Rex had taken this job, hoping it would be a nice change of pace. He'd lived a hard life up to this point—fighting in the army against the confederates and helping lead folks through the frontier to realize their dreams in the West. Working the sawmill was the simple, straightforward job he had always wanted.

Rex wandered to the tree line and found himself at the edge of a vast park, an open meadow stretched out several hundred yards across. It was beautiful to behold. The view alone was worth the hike.

The sun's light had just begun to touch the distant peaks. Steam rose off the dew-covered grass, creating an almost magical scene. Three cow elk grazed near the pines. One of the cows looked over to Rex, let out a mew, and they retreated deep into the forest.

Rex wished Abigail was with him to see it all. She would have enjoyed everything about the place. Abigail always loved being in the mountains and the forests. At least before she got sick.

Rex wiped his eyes with the sleeve of his shirt.

Working the sawmill at Summit Park was hard. The days were long, and the effort to keep things moving along could take a lot out of a man, but Rex did enjoy the scenery up here. It sure beat the sagebrush and dirt in the valley below, though some of the other men mentioned several times how they preferred the red rocks and pinyon pines.

The roll wasn't particularly tasty, but he needed to put something in his guts if he wanted the energy to make it to lunch. Rex ate the last bite before wiping the crumbs away from his greying beard. He stretched and then wandered back into the trees. It was time to finish up his work, or else he'd miss lunch.

Rex wandered around looking for trees that would be good to cut down for lumber. He was about to mark his first one when a branch snapped nearby. Rex twisted his head in the sound's direction but couldn't see anything out of the ordinary.

"Hello? Sam, is that you?"

Nobody replied.

"I swear to God, if that's you messing around, I'll beat your ass so hard you'll walk with a limp for the rest of the season!"

Sam and Rex got along just fine, but Sam had a playful streak in him. Not only that, Sam could get downright wicked if he wanted. Unfortunately, that combination wasn't always the best pair. One day, Rex had woken up to find Sam had unstitched all of Rex's pants. Emmett, their boss, was not amused.

After another few breaths, Rex still couldn't see anything. He shrugged and got back to work. It could have been a deer or an elk, as there were plenty of those up here. Hell, it could have been a bear.

A big ol' black bear had gotten into the camp kitchen a few weeks ago and made a huge mess. Needless to say, they ate bear that night for dinner.

Another branch cracked, closer this time. Rex whirled around but still couldn't see anything out of the ordinary. However, the weight of someone, or something, watching him was heavier than a wet, woolen blanket.

"Sam? Hello? Is anyone there?"

Nothing.

"You better not be playing another joke. It's not funny anymore!"

Afraid it might be a bear, Rex pulled his pistol from his holster and fired a shot up into the air.

"The next one has your name on it!"

If it was a bear, it didn't seem bothered by him or the noise. Instead, the snapping branches and footfalls continued to close the distance. Rex peered through the trees, trying to see what it was. What he saw made him nearly piss his trousers.

He fired two more shots before he turned tail and took off running.

First, his screams echoed through the forest. Then came the snap and crack of branches and bones.

Evelyn sat on a flat rock next to a babbling brook. It was dark out, but the moon was full in the night sky, giving her just enough light to see. She ran her fingers through the cool water and let her mind drift with the current.

Even though she had plenty of moments like this, moments to herself, Evelyn always took advantage of them. Life was too short to ignore the natural beauty of the world. She would know, as she had died once before in a forest not dissimilar to this one about twenty years past. If it hadn't been for Theresa Huntington, a young witch with a lot of power, Evelyn would have been nothing but a memory at this point.

She splashed some of the cold water onto her face and slicked back her red hair, marked with a noticeable white streak. The grime and sweat covering her body meant she was overdue for a bath and couldn't wait to hit the next civilized town, but there was something quite refreshing about cool mountain water as well.

"I love you."

Goosebumps broke out on her skin as she looked up from the water to find Raymond standing across the brook with his signature crooked smile. He looked pale in the moonlight, his skin almost alabaster.

"You're a fool for it," she replied.

That was always her reply because saying anything else just reignited the pain of when he had died nearly twenty years ago.

Died was putting it nicely. Raymond was murdered by an outlaw named O'Henry and then corrupted by some *thing* deep in the mountain caves. Evelyn blamed herself for it all. She should have been quicker on the draw or paid more attention before O'Henry and his men snuck up on them at their camp. There was a time, long ago, that Evelyn thought about marrying Raymond. If she could go back in time and change things, she would in a heartbeat.

Raymond sat on a tree stump, his movements stiff and jerky. He took his hat off and placed it on his knees.

"We need to talk."

"There ain't nothing to say anymore," Evelyn said, her accent slipping through. She could usually keep it in check, but it would always make an appearance when she became flustered or too excited. She knew where this was going. It always went like this. Always.

"You need to seek the truth," Raymond said.

"Not this again."

Raymond's gaze drilled into her, stirring up so many different emotions: anger, sadness... love. The tips of his snowy fingers were visible at the edge of her periphery as he clutched the bank of the creek.

"It's time to shed the lies and seek the truth."

"Stop it," Evelyn said. She closed her eyes and looked away, but somehow that made it worse, especially when Raymond crawled into the water next to her.

"Come and join us, Eve. It's nice in the darkness."

He placed a cold hand on her shoulder, and she jerked away. Evelyn scrambled backward on all fours and finally opened her eyes. Raymond crouched in the creek like he was a gargoyle. His grin had shifted into something unnatural, too wide. His face was cloaked in shadow, but one of his eyes took on an azure glow.

He sang a song he used to sing to her when the night was cold and they stared at the stars. But this version was discordant and without mirth.

Beautiful star in heav'n so bright,
Softly falls thy silv'ry light,
As thou movest from Earth afar
Star of the evening
Beautiful star

As he sang, things splashed in the water around him, whipping around and wriggling with delight. She couldn't see them clearly, but they were ropy and glistened in the moonlight.

Evelyn clenched her eyes shut. "This isn't real! None of this is real!"

The splashing stopped, and the woods became silent. When she opened her eyes, she found Raymond sitting on the side of the bank once again. His eye stopped glowing as his expression returned to normal.

This was a first.

"Eve?"

The confused tone in his voice made her start crying even harder. "Raymond, is it really you?"

He gave her a genuine smile. Then, he pointed to his eye, the one that had been glowing before. "All that strength and determination is in your eye. It's all there when you need it."

"What are you talking about? I don't understand."

He pointed to his eye again. However, as he did, his eye decomposed, shriveling up before falling out with a gout of blood.

Evelyn woke covered in sweat even though it was cold enough to see her breath forming clouds in front of her. The sun hadn't risen fully yet, but it cast enough of its rays to light up the eastern sky. Her horse, Stinker, grazed nearby.

Evelyn sat up and wiped the sweat from her brow. As she did, Stinker gave her a quiet whinny.

"Yeah, yeah, I know. We'll get moving soon."

She stood, stretched, and tried to rub some of the aches away, but sleeping on the ground was taking more and more of a toll on her body these days. At fifty years old, she wasn't as spry as she used to be.

Evelyn walked over to where her saddle lay on the ground with the rest of her gear. There was a rasher of bacon in her saddlebags and some ground coffee that would help get her going. However, she stopped short and pulled her pistol. Something wasn't right.

Evelyn looked all around but couldn't see anyone. However, someone must have been there before. Because sitting on top of her saddle, close to the Colt Navy pistol that sometimes whispered horrible things to her, was the wanted poster for Billy "The Cannibal" Hughes. That same poster had been secured deep in the bottom of her saddlebag before she had gone to sleep.

CHAPTER 1

E velyn rode her horse up a well-worn wagon trail with deep ruts cutting into the earth showing the signs of grit, determination, and hardship. Hills of red rock dotted the landscape, creating something to look at other than the sagebrush. It had its own natural beauty, but Evelyn preferred lots of trees. The sun was high in the sky, and although it was fall with winter just around the corner, it was a warm day.

She patted Stinker on the neck and was rewarded with a huff.

"Not much farther, I think. Then we can get you some nice food and water. Hell, maybe we can even get you all cleaned up and looking nice again. What do you think about that?"

Stinker shook his head and kept plodding along the trail.

"When you're right, you're right. I mean, how can I call you Stinker if you smell nice?"

If Stinker understood, he didn't show it. They continued riding until off in the distance a murder of crows circled in the air. The birds' caws cut through Evelyn's ears. Whatever they were interested in, it was maybe a quarter mile off the trail near the rocky hills.

"What do you think? Should we check it out?"

Stinker didn't reply but turned toward the birds.

"Yeah. I think so too."

Sagebrush and rocks dotted the landscape leading up to the sandstone hills. As they neared the rocks, the stink of death filled the air, and the caw of the crows grew louder. A half-dozen of the black birds sat on a rock, pecking at whatever it was they deemed their prize. Evelyn tried to see, but there were too many birds.

"Get out of here!" Evelyn said. A few of the birds hopped around, but the group was reluctant to give up their meal. Evelyn pulled her pistol and squeezed the trigger. That lit a fire underneath them, and they took off, revealing what they had been eating.

A human corpse.

Well, the remains of a human corpse anyway. Evelyn dismounted and walked over. She used a handkerchief to cover her nose and mouth, as the stink was so strong she could taste the death in the air.

The body was that of a man, though the only way she could tell was due to the wispy beard adorning the man's dried-out face. All the meat from the shoulders to the hands and the legs down to the feet were gone. The crows had picked the scraps left along the ribs and had gotten into the guts.

Somebody had neatly folded the man's clothes and placed them near the body. Next to those were his boots.

Evelyn picked up a nearby stick and poked around the insides. The heart, liver, and kidneys were gone, and upon close inspection, a sharp blade had been used to cut them out. The cut marks were clean, not ragged or torn, which would have indicated an animal.

She examined the rest of the body and found knife marks on the femur and humerus. Someone had cut the meat off the bone. Evelyn figured that someone was Billy Hughes. This fit his style.

While finding a dead body was disturbing and sad, as that person was probably somebody's family or friend, it meant she was closing in on Billy. Evelyn dropped the stick and mounted Stinker.

"Let's get going."

Stinker was all too eager to obey and trotted back to the wagon trail. As soon as they had left the area, the birds returned to finish their feast.

After another hour of travel, a procession of soldiers on horseback came into view. Evelyn urged Stinker off to the side of the trail and waited as they came closer.

The lead soldier, an older man with a grey beard and hardened eyes, tipped his hat to her as he neared.

"Ma'am."

His voice was gruff and tinged with the tired exasperation that came with age or trauma. Evelyn bet this man had experienced his share of both during his lifetime. He wore lieutenant rank on his uniform.

"Lieutenant."

The lieutenant pulled his horse, a strawberry roan, off to the side of the trail to converse with Evelyn as his soldiers continued riding along. There were about twenty of them in total, their horses laden with supplies. A rickety wagon followed at the rear, also full of food and supplies.

"Looks like you're headed out for a while," Evelyn said.

The lieutenant took his hat off and wiped the sweat off his balding head. "Indeed we are."

"I found a dead body a little farther back, might be one of yours."

Hardness crept into the man's eyes. "That is unfortunate. Might be, but we can't afford the delay. Fort Thornburgh is a little farther that way though," he said and pointed down the trail. "Perhaps you can find someone to help you there. Are you out here by yourself?"

"Yes, I am. But that's okay, I've become accustomed to the solitary lifestyle."

"This country isn't a place for a spry young woman such as yourself."

Evelyn ignored the lieutenant's attempt at flattery. It had been many years since she considered herself young or spry.

"Where are you headed?" Evelyn asked.

"Can't say, unfortunately. That's official business and all."

"Of course."

"Ma'am," he said, putting his hat back on. "You take care now."

"You as well."

Evelyn watched him ride to the front of the line before she urged Stinker back onto the trail. It wasn't long before adobe buildings dotted the landscape next to Ashely Creek. In the distance, the mighty Uintah mountains rose up like massive battlements. Several soldiers tended to the horses and other chores, no doubt to keep them busy and out of trouble. A makeshift fence surrounded the buildings, with a pair of sentries posted at the gate. Evelyn had finally arrived at Fort Thornburgh.

The guards, two men wearing faded uniforms of blue, leaned against the wooden posts and watched Evelyn with interest as she rode up to the Fort. One had a droopy eyelid and a wiry mustache. The other sported about ten days of beard growth, although it came in patchy and thin.

She tipped her hat towards them and brushed a lock of pure white hair away from her eyes. The rest of her hair was red, though greying in some areas, but the strip of white—a token of when she had nearly died twenty years ago—stood out like a polecat in a dance hall.

One of the guards spat on the ground as she passed. The other tipped his hat and mumbled, "ma'am." They undoubtedly wondered who she was, traveling by herself in such a rough country. Evelyn had encountered men like them many times before. Most chose to keep their opinions to themselves, though some weren't as smart.

Luckily, these two decided they didn't want to trouble themselves with the likes of a lone woman traveler. Evelyn counted her blessings and rode toward the stables.

A young man wearing patched wool trousers and a shirt that was maybe once white cleaned the stables. He couldn't have been more than fifteen years old and had a shaggy mop of hair. When Evelyn rode up on Stinker, the boy put his pitchfork away and ran over to her.

"That sure is a nice horse you got there. What is it, an Appaloosa?" the boy asked.

Evelyn smiled and nodded. "Indeed. I won Stinker in a poker game about five years ago."

The boy laughed. "Stinker?! That's a funny name. Fitting though," he said as he waved his hand in front of his nose. "You want me to clean him up?"

Evelyn dismounted and stretched. "That'd be lovely." She dug a few coins from her belt pouch and handed them over.

The boy's eyes lit up at the money. "That's too much, ma'am."

"Consider it a bonus if you get it done quick." The boy pocketed the money and took the reins. Evelyn looked around the fort. "Who's in charge here?"

The boy pointed over to a larger adobe building. "You'll find Captain Smith over there. He's the one to talk to. Careful though, he's a grumpy one."

"Good to know. Thank you."

The boy led Stinker into the stables and started stripping the tack off of him. Evelyn walked towards the main building, avoiding horse droppings or muddy puddles. Although in the back of her mind, she didn't know why she cared. She was just as filthy from travel as Stinker was. Evelyn needed a nice long bath and a soft bed. However, she had business to attend to first.

Soldiers eyed her with equal amounts of suspicion and desire as she meandered toward Captain Smith's building. She was something new, which always caused a stir wherever she went. Evelyn gripped her leather medicine bag, her fingers playing with the snow-white raven's feather tied to it to help calm her nerves and steady her mind.

As she neared the door, the sounds of a woman crying came from inside.

"Captain, please! Can't you spare one or two of your soldiers to go up into the mountains and look for him? He hasn't been back in nearly five days!"

Evelyn walked into the building and sat on a
rough-hewn bench made from pine in the hallway. The
captain's office was visible on the opposite side of the hallway, and it allowed Evelyn to place a face with the voice.

Inside the office, the captain sat behind a desk. He had a
blonde mustache, short hair, and an eyepatch over his left
eye. His uniform was crisp and clean, unlike most of the
other soldiers at the fort.

Sitting across from him was an older woman wearing a
plain brown dress and clutching something in her hands.
Her hair was grey and pulled up into a tight bun.

"Mrs. Francis, as I have mentioned before, I would love
nothing more than to help you. But I can't spare any of my
men at this time. With the recent Ute activity, I need every
rifle I can get here at the fort to defend the region. I'm sure
you understand?" Captain Smith said.

Mrs. Francis stood and started to say something, but
Captain Smith held a hand up and stopped her mid-sen-
tence. "I'm sure he's just up there helping out with the
sawmill and will be back any time now. Now, if you'll
please excuse me, I have business to attend to."

Tears ran down Mrs. Francis' face. She turned and left,
pausing only for a second to look at Evelyn before heading
out the door. Evelyn stood and knocked on the captain's
doorframe.

He looked up at her and smiled. "Ma'am. How can I
help you?"

Evelyn walked in and offered her hand. "I'm Evelyn Horn. I work for the Pinkerton Detective Agency."

The captain stared at her hand for a moment before shaking it with a firm grip. "A Pinkerton you say? What brings a detective so far west? A woman, nonetheless. Are you traveling alone?"

Evelyn ignored the last question. "I'm searching for Billy "The Cannibal" Hughes. I've reason to believe he's out this way." She unfolded the wanted poster and slid it across the desk.

Captain Smith glanced at the poster for a moment before pushing it back to Evelyn. "How brave of you. Billy is quite dangerous, from what I've heard. Although I don't suspect he's here. I would know."

Evelyn folded the poster back up. "I found evidence of his presence not more than an hour away from here. A body carved up and stripped of meat. If you send a couple of soldiers with me, I can lead them to it."

A look of false concern crossed the captain's face. "A body, you say? Quite terrible. Probably just the work of those Ute savages. I'm sure you overheard me talking with Mrs. Francis earlier. The Utes have started gathering their forces."

"This wasn't the work of the Utes or any other tribes. They don't dress bodies like this. No, this was the work of Billy Hughes. I know it. If you could just lend me some support, the Pinkertons wou—"

Captain Smith raised his hand, just as he had with Mrs. Francis. "I can't spare anyone at all. As you can see, I'm shorthanded."

"We crossed paths. Where are they headed?"

"That's sensitive information, I'm afraid. Army business, I'm sure you understand. My suggestion is for you to ride into town or back where you came from and let men handle these matters. I would be heartbroken to find you dead out in the woods."

Evelyn didn't let his words get to her. She was used to men underestimating her. The captain was a dead end, so she stood. Captain Smith stood as well and offered his signature smile.

"Have a good day, Captain."

"You as well, Ms. Horn."

As she walked out of the captain's office, she couldn't shake the feeling that something was amiss. What the Captain had told her didn't add up, nor did the way he brushed off the news of the body. He was hiding something.

CHAPTER 2

E velyn stepped out of the building, and Mrs. Francis'
eyes lit up. The old woman ran over to Evelyn. Her
eyes were puffy and red from crying.

"Excuse me, you said you were a Pinkerton?" Mrs. Francis asked.

"That's right. Evelyn Horn."

"I am Ursula Francis. My husband, Jackson, is missing.
Can you please help me find him?"

Evelyn's heart went out to the woman. She knew the
struggle and ache that came with a loved one who had
gone missing—countless hours of wondering, your mind
hiking down endless trails of darkness. The never knowing was the worst, because in that uncertainty, there was
always a little bit of hope, and that hope sometimes cut
deeper than loss.

However, that being said, Evelyn had her own problems
to deal with.

"I'm very sorry, Mrs. Francis. I wish I could help you, I truly do, but I'm on an important task, and I can't take on any other jobs at the moment."

It hurt Evelyn to say those words, especially when the tears began to flow again from Ursula's eyes.

"But... please! You have to help me. I can't go traipsing alone out in the wilderness. I'm not as young as I used to be, and my back prevents me from riding for longer than an hour or so. Please!"

It was hard to say no, but before Evelyn could get a word in, Ursula dug into her pocket and produced an old daguerreotype picture. Evelyn braced herself, hoping that it wasn't the remains of the man she had come across earlier.

Ursula handed it over to Evelyn. The picture itself was created on a piece of silver-laced copper and had a slight heft to it. It showed both Ursula and a man Evelyn assumed was Jackson. He wasn't the man she had found before. Evelyn let out a sigh of relief.

The picture was grainy but still showed enough detail to give Evelyn a good idea of his characteristics. Jackson had a hawkish nose and strong chin, standing a good foot taller than Ursula. They must have had the daguerreotype taken years ago, as the Ursula in the picture was much younger.

As Evelyn studied the details, Ursula produced a handkerchief and wiped her eyes.

"I warned him not to go messing around with that witch, Huntington. Nothing but trouble, I said. But would he listen? No! Now he's gone. My poor Jackson is gone!"

Evelyn's ears perked up at the mention of the name Huntington. She handed the daguerreotype back to Ursula. Could it be her dear friend, Theresa Huntington?

"Witch, you say? Does this particular witch have reddish blonde hair and blue eyes?"

Ursula gave Evelyn a confused look. "Oh, yes, the bluest eyes I've ever seen. Her hair isn't as red as yours, or what yours used to be." Ursula realized what she had just said and blushed. "I'm sorry, I didn't mean to...."

Evelyn smiled. "It's okay. Age catches up with all of us sooner or later. Please, continue," Evelyn said.

"Um, yes. She has red hair and the bluest eyes I've ever seen."

"Do you know her first name?" Evelyn asked although she knew deep down in her guts that this was, in fact, Theresa.

"Let me think... it's Tammy or...."

"Theresa?"

Ursula's eyes lit up as a meek smile crept into her lips. "Yes! That's it, Theresa. You do know her, don't you?"

Evelyn nodded.

"Where does this witch live?"

"She lives in a cabin outside of Ashely, up in the foothills just before the mountains get too steep. If you follow the Carter military road towards the mountain, you'll come to a split. Her cabin is just a ways up that split."

Evelyn's mind raced with the thought of seeing her dear friend again. It had been over ten years since she saw her last.

"Thank you. I think I'll pay her a visit." Before Evelyn left, she put a hand on Ursula's shoulder. "I'll keep an eye out for Jackson, and I'll ask about him when I visit Ms. Huntington."

More tears flowed from Ursula's eyes. "Thank you! Thank you so much! Here, take this with you."

She handed Evelyn the daguerreotype. Although Evelyn tried to give it back, Ursula wouldn't have any of it.

"You can give it back when you find him. You are an angel from heaven, Ms. Horn."

Evelyn's face flushed as she looked to the ground. "I don't know about that. And no promises."

Ursula patted Evelyn's shoulder and looked like she wanted to hug the woman. "Of course, of course. Thank you. You're the first person who has offered to help me at all."

Evelyn tipped her hat to Ursula and made her way to the stables, but Ursula called out to her before she got too far.

"You be careful out there. That witch is dangerous."

"Probably more than you know," Evelyn replied.

When she got back to the stables, the stable boy was still in the process of cleaning up Stinker.

"About how much longer do you reckon?" Evelyn asked.

The boy looked up from his duties and smiled. "Oh, no more than thirty minutes."

"Make it twenty, and you can have this," Evelyn said and held up another coin.

The boy's grin got even bigger. "You got it, ma'am!"

Evelyn walked around Fort Thornburgh. She halfway considered taking Stinker now and riding out to Theresa's cabin, but it seemed a waste to stop the stable boy from his duties. Plus, she hadn't seen Theresa in so many years. Another twenty minutes wouldn't make a big difference.

Evelyn decided to look around the fort and strolled out into the main thoroughfare, not that the fort itself was very big. A message board stood near one of the buildings, and dozens of notes, missives, and pictures decorated the board. After a quick inspection, Evelyn found they all regarded missing persons.

There were surprisingly many for such a tiny area. It further cemented her suspicion that Captain Smith was up to something, and he knew more than he let on.

Evelyn watched what the soldiers were doing. There appeared to be a small contingent of them gathering gear up as if they were ready to ride out, which didn't make sense if what Captain Smith said was true. Didn't he need every able-bodied man here to defend the region from the Utes?

She walked past two soldiers who eyed her as she passed. One sported curly hair and a pair of mutton chops. He dunked his head into a barrel of water and washed his face. The other was tall, lean, and had a visage that reminded Evelyn of a rodent. They fell into step behind her, and within two heartbeats, they flanked her on either side.

"What happened to your hair?" Mutton Chops asked.

"Don't you two have chorin' to do?" Evelyn asked.

"We can't talk about Army business to the common layperson such as yourself," Rodent Face said.

"Yeah, it's secret. Now, I ain't ever seen a redhead with a skunk stripe like you. What happened? You see a ghost?" Mutton Chops asked. He reached a hand up to touch her hair. His mistake.

Evelyn grabbed the man's wrist and twisted. He let out a grunt of pain and dropped to his knees. He tried to move away, but the way Evelyn put pressure on his wrist made that impossible without going through a lot of pain. It was a neat trick she had picked up in Ogden.

Rodent Face moved forward, but Evelyn was quicker, drawing her pistol with a smooth motion and pointing it right at his rat snout.

Rodent Face put his hands up and took a step back. "Fiesty, aren't we?"

Evelyn pulled the hammer back on her pistol in reply.

"Shit! You're breaking my wrist!" Mutton Chops yelled.

Evelyn let him go but kicked him away before taking a big step back, putting some distance between her and Rodent Face.

"I suggest you attend to those secret army chores," she said.

Rodent Face smiled, but his eyes promised darker things. Mutton Chops got to his feet and nursed his wrist. He shot her a look that stunk worse than an outhouse on a hot summer day.

The pair didn't move for a moment, but Rodent Face finally pulled his friend away and they wandered back to the water barrel. Evelyn decided she had overstayed her welcome as a few other soldiers began to eye her after the exchange.

She walked back to the stable and was happy to see the boy tightening the strap of her saddle on Stinker. Evelyn mounted her horse and flipped the promised coin to the kid.

"Thank you, ma'am!" The boy admired the coin before pocketing it. Then, he pointed to the large pistol on her saddle. "That sure is a fancy gun."

"Fancy isn't the right word. Maybe damned or cursed would be a better one. You didn't touch it, did you?"

The whispers slithered into her ear, as merely talking about the weapon had woken it from whatever slumber it had. Evelyn gripped the medicine pouch around her neck, and the whispers subsided.

The boy shook his head.

"No, ma'am. We're told not to mess with anything that don't need messin' with."

"Good."

Evelyn spun Stinker around and rode out of the front gate at a quick trot. Once she was away from the fort, she made sure nobody followed her. Satisfied, she started toward the town of Ashely.

The road leading up into the mountains was easy enough to find. It took her up into the hills, and soon enough, Ashely and Fort Thornburgh were out of sight and out of mind.

In the distance, a large, rocky cliff of red rock and iron-infused sand towered into the sky. Sage and juniper dotted the landscape. The turnoff that Ursula talked about appeared ahead. Evelyn took the turn and headed further up into the hills. Not long after, Theresa's cabin came into view.

It was a tiny little thing, probably just a couple of rooms. The roof sagged, and the foliage had begun to reclaim its land. The windows were covered with dust and grime, and the tiny little fence out front had seen better days. The planks were warped and sun-blasted, and entire sections were missing. In short, it was a perfect witch house.

Feelings of joy and trepidation about seeing her long-lost friend disappeared when Evelyn rode closer. The door to the cabin hung on its side, one hinge trying its best to keep it from falling over. Someone had kicked that door in.

CHAPTER 3

Evelyn dismounted Stinker and drew her pistol. The Colt Navy still sat in its home on her saddle, and for half a moment, she thought about taking it with her. The sultry voice of the weapon slithered into her ear.

You never know what you might find in a witch's house. Best be protected.

Evelyn shivered. She grabbed onto the leather pouch at her neck, forcing the voice to fade away. Then, leaving the Colt Navy in its holster, Evelyn crept up to the cabin's entrance and peered in.

At first glance, it was hard to tell if anyone was there, but Evelyn couldn't detect any movement. She pushed the door open a little more and revealed a horrifying scene.

The cabin interior was a mess. The table was overturned, bedding strewn about, all the contents from every drawer and container were scattered across the floor.

"Theresa? You here?" Evelyn's voice cracked as she called out, still unsure whether she should be stealthy or if that bird had flown already.

If there was someone here, they had to know Evelyn was around by now. She stepped into the cabin, and a slight electric tingle crept up her spine. A quick glance at the threshold revealed her assumptions.

A series of sigils and bind runes were carved into the wood using the old Germanic Elder Futhark system. Theresa had tried many times to teach Evelyn how to use sigils and runes for magic, but Evelyn's skills with the arcane were downright embarrassing. However, she did have enough talent to feel power when it was around, hence the tingle.

Those runes above the doorway were meant to keep out negative energy and evil spirits, which meant whatever had come into this cabin was human or very strong. Evelyn had seen Theresa's protection spells stop a charging hellhound right in its tracks as if it had hit a stone wall.

Evelyn took care not to step on anything, cautiously picking her steps as she made her way through the tiny cabin. The cabin interior, much like the exterior, had seen better days, and it wasn't due to the ransacking. There were gaps in the walls, the bed lay at a strange angle, and the fireplace needed some help. Yet, despite the mess and rundown nature of it all, there was still a sense of home here. Evelyn almost smiled as she pictured what it looked like before someone had torn the place apart.

"You were doing all right for yourself, weren't you, kid?"

Evelyn picked the table up off the floor, set it upright, and started to clean up some of the papers. The first one she found was a hand-drawn map of the area with what appeared to be the Carter military road leading up into the mountains nearby. A large X sat next to a spot near the top that said, Summit Park. Evelyn recognized the handwriting as Theresa's.

"Okay, kid. What were you looking for?"

Nothing else on the map indicated what was at the X, though. Evelyn held the paper up to the light to ascertain if there were any other markings she couldn't see, but it appeared that it was simply just a map.

She grabbed some more papers off the ground, recipes for different tinctures and poultices, and revealed a dark spot on the floor. It was blood.

Evelyn hoped it wasn't Theresa's, but deep down, she knew it was. Luckily, it wasn't a lot.

"What happened here?"

Evelyn continued her search for clues but came up short. Everything scattered across the floor was clothing, bedding, dried herbs and ingredients, a set of runes carved into pieces of elk antler... but nothing that would help Evelyn figure out who took Theresa or where. So far, the only lead she had was the map to Summit Park.

"Looks like we're headed up into the mountains again."

Evelyn turned to leave, but before she could take two steps, something slid off the wall and hit the floor behind her. She spun, pointing her pistol, but nobody was there. A quick search revealed it was an old tintype photo that had fallen.

The photo was of Theresa and Evelyn. Evelyn sat on a chair while Theresa stood behind her. It was one of the rare occasions Evelyn had put on a dress and cleaned up outside of disguise and costumes for work. Theresa even sported the pearl hairclip Evelyn had given her on her 21st birthday.

She remembered that day well. They had come into Salt Lake City to clean up, resupply, and get some well-needed rest before heading back out into the wilderness. Instead of staying for only a night, they remained in Salt Lake for three, and everything was great for a short moment in time. There weren't things in the shadows stalking them. There weren't unknown truths that could shatter a person's soul. There was just Theresa and Evelyn.

They had eaten so much food one of the days that Theresa got sick to her stomach and ended up throwing up a lot of it later that night. But even that was a fond memory because nobody was trying to kill them.

Theresa had asked her at one point during that respite why they didn't just stop searching the shadows for esoteric things and fighting the darkness. She mentioned they could have a life in Salt Lake City, and she was serious. There was a part of Evelyn that wanted to do that. It was a nice dream, but it *was* just a dream. Evelyn had asked her, if they didn't fight that darkness, who would? Plus, if there was any way to get Raymond back, to erase that horrible memory, she would find it.

Evelyn crouched down and picked the tintype up. Her fingers brushed across something on the back. She flipped it around and found a small bundle of papers tied with twine. The bundle was secured to the tintype with melted wax.

She broke the wax bond and untied the twine. The first thing was an old paper that felt as if it could break apart and turn to dust at any moment. It was written in what appeared to be Latin. Evelyn knew a little Latin, but not enough to make any sense of the document... something about many eyes and the trees.

The second paper was a translation of the first, written in Theresa's handwriting. It read:

When the stars danced and the moon turned to blood, a dark star fell to the earth. With it came death. The Sorcerers of the Worm bound the creature to the trees deep in the ground. From that moment forward, it was no longer itself. It was the Root of a Thousand Eyes.

The trees will mute its power and keep it slumbering.

Full moon. Aspens?

Seven shall stand when the moon is brimming. Their hearts offered to awaken/summon/bring forth the branches?

Do you seek the truth?

There it was again. That damned phrase about the truth. She had first come across it twenty years ago in the town of Fairfield, where the one-eyed woman and the crazed Colonel with the wooden hand had tried to kill Evelyn and her partner, Raymond. Since that day, she had come across that phrase too many times to count, yet to date, she had only glimpsed the truth and it had nearly killed her. Technically, it *had* killed her. Theresa had to rip her soul back from the land of the dead and shove it back into Evelyn's body.

The following paper was old, somehow older than the first. Whatever it was, was written in a language that Evelyn didn't recognize. Evelyn shook her head and flipped to the final page. The last paper was a list of seven names in total, the first being Captain Marcus Smith. Evelyn didn't recognize any of the others except the last, which was Jackson Francis.

Perhaps Evelyn needed to pay Ursula a visit. Obviously, there was more going on than the kind old woman had told her.

Evelyn sighed, pocketed the papers, and placed the tintype back on the wall. What was Theresa caught up in? Nothing good, to be sure.

She was about to step out the door when she heard voices in the distance. A moment later, two horsemen came into view riding towards the cabin.

"Shit."

Evelyn thought about hopping on Stinker and riding away, but the other riders were close enough that they would surely see her. The time to make a decision dwindled as the riders closed in on the cabin.

CHAPTER 4

E velyn sneaked out the back window as quietly as she could, taking care not to step on any stray branches out the back. She thought about whistling for Stinker now that she was out of the cabin, but the riders were closing in fast.

"Hey, who's horse is that?" a man asked.

"How the fuck should I know?" the other answered.

Evelyn cursed her luck and drew her pistol. There was no backing out now. She peeked around the corner to get a better look at who they were.

The two riders wore plain clothes but sported beat-up cavalry hats. Evelyn knew them. It was Mutton Chops and Rodent Face—out here on the good captain's orders, no doubt.

The pair stopped just outside of the cabin, still on their horses. Mutton Chops drew his pistol. Evelyn ducked behind the cabin again, her heart racing. She might be able to get the drop on one, but dealing with both coming from two different directions would be difficult and dangerous.

A couple of dull thuds told her they had dismounted. Evelyn silently cursed, thinking of them rummaging around in the saddle bags or messing with the Colt Navy.

"What are we looking for anyway? We already ransacked this place. Nothing but smelly plants and weird things in jars." Rodent Face asked.

"Captain Smith says we need to look again and try and find those fucking ritual papers. Without them, that damn witch can't do her magic or whatever the hell it is she does. He told me not to come back until we find them, or he'll eat our livers for dinner with a side of onions."

Rodent Face laughed at that, but his laughter died a few moments later. "You think he was Joshin' us?"

"You ever hear Captain Smith make a joke?" Mutton Chops asked.

"Nope."

"Well, there you go."

These two were here before. That meant they probably knew where Theresa was. That also meant she couldn't just kill them outright.

"Now come on, let's search this place. We'll tear up the floorboards if we have to," Mutton Chops said.

"What about the rider?" Rodent Face asked.

"Oh, yeah. Hey, you in there, come on out! We won't hurt you, I promise."

"Yeah, we're with the Army!" Rodent Face said.

Evelyn stayed quiet. Soon, the sound of boots on wood hit her ears, telling her they had entered the cabin.

"This place is just like we left it," Mutton Chops said.

"Yeah. But someone is here, no doubt about that. That horse didn't just wander here all by its lonesome."

"Show yourself! We just want to talk," Mutton Chops shouted.

Evelyn started to sneak around the cabin. As she turned the corner, her boot caught a rock, and she fell forward, her shoulder slamming into the cabin's wall. Not a breath later, a bullet hole ripped through the wall, nearly taking her face off. Evelyn hit the dirt as more bullets punched through the cabin.

The firing stopped, and Evelyn saw the cabin itself was raised. She hadn't noticed before when she had ridden up. Evelyn didn't hesitate and crawled under the structure just as the pair ran outside.

Their boots kicked up more of that red dust that was so prevalent in the region as they both went around opposite sides of the cabin. Evelyn watched them while lying on her belly. She used her elbows to turn herself around as the pair met on the backside.

"Where the fuck did they go?" Mutton Chops asked.

"I don't know. Do I look like some sort of magician?"

Eventually, they would figure out she was under the cabin, and Evelyn didn't want to lose the element of surprise. She took aim at the shin of one of them, pulled the hammer back, and squeezed the trigger.

The gun blast was much louder in the enclosed space and instantly set her ears ringing. However, she could still hear the scream of Mutton Chops as he fell to the ground, clutching his shattered leg.

Evelyn didn't waste any time. She aimed and shot, hitting Rodent Face in the boot. He dropped like a sack of potatoes, and somehow his howl was even worse than Mutton Chop's. However, unlike his compatriot, Rodent Face rolled to face her. His eyes went wide when he registered who had just shot them.

"It's that red-headed bitch from befo—"

Rodent Face didn't get a chance to finish his thought as a bullet ripped through his skull, decorating the rocks and sagebrush with bits of brain and bone.

Mutton Chops finally gathered his senses and tried to grab his gun which lay next to him, but Evelyn whistled at him to get his attention. She had her pistol pointed between his eyes.

"Don't even think about it, or I'll add an orifice to your face, just like your friend there," Evelyn said.

She crawled out from under the cabin, keeping Mutton Chops at gunpoint the entire time. Sweat and tears poured down his face as he grimaced in pain and writhed in the dirt.

"You even blink strangely, and I'll shoot your god-damned eye out," Evelyn said.

Eve, all that strength and determination is in your eye. It's all in your eye.

It was Raymond's voice, nothing more than a whisper on the wind, but as real and serious as having no water in the desert. Evelyn took a deep breath and refocused. The ringing in her ears was still there but had died down to a dull thrum.

She kicked Mutton Chop's gun away and rolled the man onto his back. He screamed in pain and tried to push her away, but Evelyn hit him in the face with the butt end of the gun.

"Struggle again, and it will be a bullet, understand?"

Mutton Chops didn't say anything but continued to howl.

Evelyn hit him again. "Do. You. Understand?"

"Yes, goddamn it! You broke my fucking leg, you bitch."

Evelyn stepped on his mangled shin, eliciting a pitiful, pain-fueled wail from the man.

"Call me bitch again, and I'll feed you your severed cock. Now listen up. You're going to answer some questions. What's this ritual you two morons were talking about?"

She let up the pressure on his leg. Mutton Chops sobbed for a moment before puking up bile onto his chest.

"You have no idea what you're getting into," he said.

"Well then, why don't you enlighten me. The ritual papers, what are they? Where is Theresa?"

Mutton Chops lay on his back, staring at the sky. He wiped his mouth and tried to slow his breathing down.

"Hey! Get to talking or else..."

"I ain't telling you shit. The captain will kill me if he finds out I told you anything."

Evelyn crouched next to him and put the gun next to his temple. "I'll kill you if you don't talk, and I'll make it slow and painful. Now spill your guts, or I will."

Something shifted in Mutton Chop's eyes. There was a fear there, a deep-rooted fear that was more primal than anything else.

"There ain't nothing you can do that would even come close to the kind of torture the captain can put on a man..." A glint of perverted glee glimmered in his eye for just a moment. "...or a woman. He's got your witch. But she says she can't do a thing without the papers."

Evelyn poked his shin with the barrel of her pistol. Mutton Chops screamed and thrashed away from her.

"Where is she?" Evelyn asked.

"She's with the captain. He's got ways of making someone talk."

Evelyn's blood boiled at the thought of Captain Smith touching Theresa and hurting her. He just earned a bullet from the Colt Navy on her saddle. Just thinking about using the gun made her skin break out with goosebumps, but it would be worth making him pay.

"He's gonna have fun with you too," Mutton Chops said with a smile.

"I'd worry about yourself right now," Evelyn said and stood. "You know, the coyotes out here get mighty hungry this time of year."

Mutton Chops winced in pain. He looked at her with one open eye. "What the fuck are you talking about?"

"Food gets scarce... but did you know coyotes can smell blood from a mile away?"

Mutton Chops looked around before propping himself up on his elbows. "There ain't no coyotes around."

Evelyn smiled. "Not yet."

She shot him in the other leg. Blood spurt from the wound, and he clutched his leg, screaming.

"What the fuck?"

Then she shot him in the arm. Then in the other arm.

"They'll be around soon enough."

Evelyn took his pistol and Rat Face's weapon as well. Then, she left him there crying and wallowing in his own blood.

Evelyn had to go see the captain and talk to him about some things.

CHAPTER 5

Evelyn rode through the gate of Fort Thornburgh at a brisk pace. One lone soldier slumped against the wall woke as she rode by. He ordered her to stop but lacked the motivation to do anything other than shout expletives.

While it was night, there was a distinct lack of people in the fort. Other than a couple of guards wandering the perimeter and the fool at the gate, the place appeared empty. They might have been asleep, but a quick glance at the nearly empty livery told her they were gone.

She urged Stinker over to Captain Smith's office and hopped off, not even bothering to hitch him to the post. She might have to make a fast getaway, and seconds could mean the difference between life and death.

Evelyn expected some resistance, so she drew her pistol and stormed inside. The first thing she noticed was the lack of soldiers or people of any kind. From where she stood in the hallway, there wasn't a soul. The building itself wasn't big—only Captain Smith's office and two other rooms.

Evelyn kicked the captain's door open and ran in, ready to unleash hell on anyone who wanted to stop her. However, the captain wasn't there. She spun around, expecting soldiers to start storming in... but there was nobody.

She felt stupid for barging in like an angry bison. Evelyn was better than that. But her emotions were starting to get the better of her.

With her gun still out and ready, Evelyn walked to the desk and rummaged through the leaf of papers. She found discipline reports, logistics, supply requests, and even a fairly detailed report on the status of the local Ute tribes, but nothing of interest to her. The reports were hardly a prediction of the upcoming Armageddon that Captain Smith made the Utes out to be.

Evelyn sat in the chair and opened up one of the two desk drawers. The top drawer contained blank paper, ink, writing implements, and a letter opener. The second drawer was locked.

Evelyn searched for the key but couldn't find it anywhere. More than likely, Captain Smith had it on his person. However, Evelyn wasn't about to let a little thing like a locked drawer stand in her way. She took her hat off and pulled her hairpin, which allowed her fiery hair to fall across her back and shoulders. The hairpin doubled as a dagger and had saved her on many occasions. It also served as a great lockpick.

She fumbled with the lock for a few minutes before finally hitting things exactly how they needed to be hit, and the mechanism unlocked with a subtle click. Evelyn pulled the drawer open, and a small, silver flask slid forward, hitting the inside wall. She opened up the top and sniffed—whiskey. Not wanting to let it go to waste, Evelyn took a swig and then put the flask in her coat pocket.

Aside from the flask, the drawer contained two items. The first was a leatherbound book that looked like a journal or diary of some sort. However, the second item caught her attention: Theresa's pearl hairclip. The exact one from the tintype.

Evelyn knew that hairclip like it was her own, as she had seen it on Theresa for many years. Tears welled up in Evelyn's eyes as the thought of Captain Smith and his soldiers torturing Theresa entered her mind. She gripped the hairclip so hard it left angry red indentations in her palm and threatened to break the skin.

Evelyn vowed to find Theresa and make the captain pay for his sins. She placed the hairclip on the desk and pulled the journal out. A long cord of soft buckskin kept the book secure. She untied it and opened it to the first page. A few loose papers spilled out, but she let them fall to the desk as something inside the book caught her eye.

Staring back at her was a sketch of a grove of aspens, but instead of the dark knots that decorated the length of the trees, they were eyes. It was a crude drawing, but the weight of those eyes bore through her soul. They offered her the truth—she knew it deep down in the darkness of her very being.

Evelyn flipped to the next page. This page had words on it, but in the same language she had found at Theresa's. Instead of letters, she saw what appeared to be small symbols or sigils in their place. It hurt her head to stare at them too long. Aside from the strange words, there were more drawings. This time, instead of the trees, the pictures depicted all sorts of body mutilations. Pages upon pages showed her how to flay skin and remove fingers or whole limbs. There were even five entire pages dedicated to the removal of an eyeball.

The page showed an intricate drawing of what appeared to be a wooden hand with odd symbols carved into it. Evelyn had seen this hand before. She had taken it off the body of Col. Green in the town of Fairfield nearly twenty years ago.

Scrawled in English next to the drawing was a name: Jackson Francis.

The rest of the pages were blank. Evelyn closed the journal and set it down on the desk before picking up the loose papers that had fallen from the book when she opened it up. The papers turned out to be a map of the area. She recognized it from the map she had found at Theresa's cabin. It showed the nearby mountains and the sawmill.

However, it also depicted an area to the southwest next to a small creek. That area was circled in red.

Evelyn wasn't sure what to make of it all. Hopefully, that's where Captain Smith had taken Theresa, but Evelyn wasn't about to charge in without more information. There was one person nearby who knew more than she had let on.

Ursula Francis.

Evelyn grabbed the journal, the map, and Theresa's hairclip before leaving. As she turned into the hallway, she ran into a portly soldier with a tired expression. The man's eyes went wide as he saw her, and he opened his mouth to shout. Evelyn punched the man in the throat, stopping the words before they could ever form.

The soldier dropped his rifle and clutched his neck, trying to breathe. Evelyn wasted no time. She drew her pistol and hit him in the face with the butt of the gun. The soldier fell to the ground, writhing on the floor and trying to breathe. He tried to get back up, but she kicked him again in the head, knocking him out cold.

"Sorry about that. I can't have you raising the alarm," she said and walked out of the building.

Stinker neighed at her when she stepped out.

"Yeah, I saw him. Thanks for the warning," Evelyn said.

Stinker shook his head and huffed. Evelyn mounted him, and they rode out of the fort the same way they entered, with a soldier throwing curses at her.

She didn't care, though. She had to pay a visit to Ursula Francis.

CHAPTER 6

Evelyn pushed Stinker hard on her way to Ursula's house. Finding out where the woman lived took a little bit of intimidation and a lot of finesse, but eventually, she found someone willing to part with the information.

While Evelyn assumed the woman lived in the town of Ashley, Ursula actually dwelled on the outskirts. Not as far as Theresa, but still far enough away that Ursula and Jackson Francis could easily keep to themselves.

By the time Ursula's home came into view, the moon was bright in the sky. It wasn't quite full, but Evelyn gave it a night, maybe two at the most before it was. That didn't give her much time to find Theresa before Captain Smith started the ritual.

Coyotes howled in the distance, and Evelyn wondered if they had found the meal she had left them at Theresa's cabin. The thought of Rat Face and Mutton Chops was enough to get her going again. That doubled with the fact that Ursula possibly had withheld information from her put Evelyn in a dour mood as she rode towards the tiny home.

Tiny was perhaps an understatement. Theresa's cabin was tiny. The Francis home was nothing more than maybe an oversized shed. Evelyn had come across outhouses that were almost as big. It couldn't be anything more than a room with a fireplace and bed.

A rickety fence lined the property, keeping about a half-a-dozen goats and cattle within its confines. A chicken coop with a sagging roof sat next to the house. Next to that was a small corral with an old paint grazing on the grass.

Evelyn jumped Stinker over the fence and stormed towards the house. Smoke came from the chimney, lazily floating into the night air, and a flickering light came from inside.

"Ursula Francis!" Evelyn called.

She dismounted Stinker, hitched him to a post, and stormed to the door. Evelyn knocked so hard that for half a second, she thought it might bust in.

"Ursula! Open up, it's Evelyn Horn!"

The light shifted inside, and soon enough, the door creaked open, revealing a tired-looking Ursula. Her grey hair framed her withered face as she looked up at Evelyn with eyes that bore the signs of crying.

"Did you find him? Did you find my Jackson?" Ursula looked past Evelyn, searching for Jackson.

The hairs on the back of Evelyn's neck rose as the distinct feeling of someone watching her washed across her body. She looked back but only saw the shadowy shapes of junipers, sage, and a lone leafless tree that stood as a sentinel in the foothills.

"Can I come inside?" Evelyn asked. Her tone was still sharp and ready to cut, but actually coming face to face with Ursula and seeing her in an obvious emotional state of being had tempered Evelyn's rage. "I have some questions."

Ursula's expression dropped from hopeful to heartbroken in an instant. "So, you haven't found him then?"

"No, I haven't, but I think I may know where he is."

That feeling of being watched became heavier. Evelyn looked back over her shoulder again but couldn't see anything. Although the lone tree seemed to have gotten closer. It was probably just her nerves doubled with lack of sleep.

Some of the cattle started to scream and ran across the yard. Ursula held up her lantern, its light shedding some of the darkness. She looked past Evelyn and shivered.

"Of course, come in, come in."

Ursula opened the door wide for Evelyn. The inside of the cabin looked bigger than the outside, though Evelyn's suspicions were correct. There was a small wood-burning stove with an iron tea kettle on top, a bed just big enough for two, and a wooden table and chairs that had seen better days.

Ursula shut the door behind Evelyn and shuffled over to the stove. The door screeched in protest when she opened it to put in another piece of wood. Before she closed it, Ursula warmed her hands by the fire.

"It's so cold out. Won't be long before the snow falls," Ursula said. "Tea?"

She poured a cup for herself and held the kettle expectantly. Evelyn shook her head, hardly paying attention to Ursula as she scanned the home for any clues or anything that could help indicate just how much Ursula knew or was involved with. However, the cabin looked like any other typical house, and without giving it a thorough search, Evelyn came up short.

"Probably better. It's chamomile tea. I can't sleep too well these days since Jackson went missing."

Evelyn decided it was best to get right to the point. "How is Jackson involved with Captain Smith, and what is he really doing up in the mountains?"

Ursula dropped her teacup. It shattered when it hit the ground, sending pieces of porcelain skittering across the floor. She sat down on the edge of the bed and began to cry again.

"So, that's where he is. I told him not to go up there. Said it was bad business. No amount of money or power is worth damning your soul."

Evelyn's brash bravado deflated. Ursula wasn't some devious antagonist in this whole thing; instead, she was a victim. She walked over to the crying woman and sat down next to her, putting an arm around Ursula's shoulder.

"Tell me everything you know. Please."

Ursula wiped her face, though it did little good. "Living out here is tough, you know? We came from Salt Lake City about four years ago, hoping to build a better life for ourselves. Big dreams about starting a ranch, but as you saw, we barely have enough livestock to eke out a living," Ursula said and pointed toward the window. "I think Jackson felt somehow responsible for the whole thing, like it was his idea, and the fact that we are only just surviving out here is all on him.

"Well, one day, he sold some of the cows to Captain Smith. When he came back, he was a different man. Smith had told him something... sold him on some sort of damned idea to get power and riches. I tried to tell him you can't make deals with the devil and not get burned. But he wouldn't listen."

Evelyn pulled the drawing of the wooden hand out of her pocket and showed it to Ursula. "Does this mean anything to you? It has his name on it."

Ursula looked at the drawing and then pushed it back to Evelyn. "You put that away now. Better yet, you should just burn the damned thing. My poor Jackson talked on and on about that hand, saying he was the one who was going to carve it. That his work would help open the door... whatever that meant. He wouldn't work on it here, though. He told me he had a special place up in the mountains to do that. He'd go up there from time to time, always coming back like he was half-starved or sick. I could see what it was doing to him. I begged him not to go anymore, saying we were doing just fine. But he didn't listen. Then, one day he didn't come back."

Carve it? If they had to make a new one, that meant Theresa didn't give up the one Evelyn had taken from Col. Green so long ago. If Theresa had been smart, she would have gotten rid of the thing. The fact that Capt. Smith needed another one didn't bode well.

"What about Theresa?"

"Who?"

"The witch. How was she involved? Did they take her up into the mountains as well?"

Ursula's face went dark. "Oh no, did they take that poor woman too? I never agreed with what she did, practicing black magic and all, but she seemed nice enough. She even gave me a tincture for my cold. Never used it, of course, but it was a kind gesture. I kept trying to get her to come to church and leave all that blasphemy behind her."

"Ursula, focus! Did they take her up into the mountains?"

"I... I don't know. I'm sorry."

The goats and cows started to scream outside. Then, the tea set on the table began to rattle. It was slight at first, just background noise, but then it got louder and louder.

Evelyn looked over and saw the entire table trembling. A picture frame fell off the wall, the glass shattering as it hit.

"Is it an earthquake?" Ursula asked. The old woman clutched the bedpost, looking wide-eyed around the cabin.

Then it stopped, and the only sound in the house was the pop of the fire and the cries of the animals outdoors. Evelyn stood, causing the bedframe to groan as she moved. She walked over to the window and found the livestock bunched up at the corner of the fence.

There was a loud snap of wood outside as if a tree had fallen. Evelyn peered through the window but couldn't see anything.

"What was that?" Ursula asked as she got up and padded over next to her.

"I don't know."

A coldness crept into Evelyn's spine, spreading into her guts—something wasn't right. Evelyn drew her pistol and continued to look outside. Ursula tied her robes tighter about her body and headed toward the front door.

"Ursula, wait! Don't op—"

It was too late. Ursula opened the door and peered out into the darkness. "Jackson, is that you?"

Evelyn couldn't see who she was talking to, but a second later, Ursula let out a scream. It was primal and full of terror.

Evelyn watched in horror as Ursula was ripped through the doorway faster than humanly possible. Her screams echoed through the night as something dragged her out into the pasture.

CHAPTER 7

Evelyn raced out the front door to find Ursula on the
ground next to the lone tree. Even though it was
dark, the woman's bloody neck glistened in the moonlight.

"Ursula!"

The tree moved and looked straight at Evelyn. Yellow
eyes that shined like a cat's stared back at her, and that's
when she realized it wasn't a tree at all.

The thing was tall, bulky, and had a set of antlers that
branched off its head like some sort of deer or elk but was
something altogether alien. It growled at Evelyn and then
crouched down low, its body cracking and creaking as if it
were a tree in the wind. Evelyn stared in horror as it opened
its mouth wide and bit down on Ursula's shoulder.

Ursula let out a shriek of pain that cut off mid-scream as
blood filled her throat. Evelyn was frozen; her mind flashed
back to a similar creature that had crawled out of the forest
many years ago. But the thing from before was a shadowy

being, and it had *killed* Evelyn as it bore through her soul like a rabid dog.

She snapped back to the present, shaking the memory off with a shiver. Evelyn aimed her pistol and shot. The bullet smacked the thing in the side with a brutal thwack, causing it to let out a small grunt of pain, but it otherwise ignored the gunshot.

She aimed again, careful not to shoot too close to Ursula, and squeezed the trigger. The gun barked, and once again, the bullet hit close to where the previous bullet had landed.

Again, it groaned but continued to rip and tear into Ursula, who gurgled in pain on the ground beneath it. Evelyn walked toward the beast and fanned her gun. Four more shots rang out into the night, and each one slapped into the monster. The final bullet hit one of its antlers, breaking a chunk off.

It snapped its head toward Evelyn and roared, sounding like a bear, cougar, and human all mixed together. Then, it dropped Ursula's body and bounded off into the night. Evelyn thought about grabbing the Colt Navy off the saddle and making chase; however, Ursula let out a pitiful gasp.

Evelyn ran over to her but knew right away it was too late. Ursula was dead. She just didn't know it yet.

The old woman looked up at Evelyn with bloodshot eyes wider than the moon. She reached out, and Evelyn grasped the woman's hand, holding it tight.

"It's too late," Ursula said before coughing up a glob of blood.

Evelyn stayed with Ursula until the woman stopped breathing. A couple of ravens landed nearby. One stared at Evelyn for a moment before letting out a soft caw.

Evelyn turned to the raven. "Do your job then; take her soul to the afterlife."

Theresa had told her when they had first met that the birds ushered the souls of the dead to their final destination. Evelyn hadn't believed it at first, but she wasn't sure what to think anymore after dying and coming back from the other side.

The raven hopped closer to Ursula's body, then both birds took off and flapped away. Evelyn watched them go, wondering if the story was true. Once they were out of sight, she found the lantern, turned it on, and returned to the scene.

The creature's tracks were massive but shaped somewhat like human feet, oddly enough. She found bits of what looked like bark lying on the ground but no blood other than Ursula's. Evelyn widened her search, and then she saw the chunk of antler she had shot off.

Evelyn picked it up. It was heavy, maybe a pound or more just in that small chunk. The exterior looked like a tree branch, but the inside was a pithy, almost honey-comb-like structure of bone that looked more akin to elk or deer.

She sniffed it and gagged. It stunk of death and rot.

Evelyn flung the bit of antler away before walking back into the house. Her next destination was Summit Park and the sawmill, but she would be remiss if she didn't look for clues or supplies in the house. There had to be something of use.

A small part of her knew it was wrong to steal from a dead woman and her husband, but the practical part knew it was the smart thing to do. She only had a day or two's worth of rations in her saddlebag. Evelyn had no idea just how long she would be up in the mountains. Sure, she knew how to forage and hunt, but those activities took time. Time was a commodity she couldn't waste.

The first place Evelyn searched was the cupboards. She found some bread, a hunk of cheese that wasn't too moldy, and some dried meat. There wasn't much else of use that she could take as far as food or drink, though.

Next, she rifled through a footlocker and the night-stand. Other than clothes, an old dress that looked like it could be a family heirloom, and some old pictures of what Evelyn assumed was perhaps Ursula's mother or grand-mother, there was nothing else of note.

Evelyn sighed in frustration and sat on the bed. Her weight shifted the bedframe, pushing it into the wall. The bedpost made a hollow thunk as it hit, catching Evelyn's attention.

She moved over to the wall and pushed the bed out of the way. Closer inspection of the spot revealed a fine outline of some sort of opening. It was nearly invisible, and Evelyn could only see it very close. Whoever made it must have been a master craftsman.

Finding no visible switches or way to open it, Evelyn pushed against the opening. A small click sounded from the other side of the wall, and when she let up the pressure, a portion of the wall had pushed out. She grabbed it with the tips of her fingers and opened it like a tiny door.

Inside was a small space about half the size of a hatbox. The only thing inside was a bundle of something wrapped up with buckskin and tied off with rawhide. Evelyn pulled it out and untied the rawhide. When she opened up the buckskin, she found a book. The book's cover was made from bark, though it appeared somewhat fleshy. Evelyn ran her fingers across it, expecting to find rough edges, but instead it was soft and warm. It made her shudder.

She opened up the first page and read.

Capt. Smith took me to the meadow today, and I saw it with my own eyes. Dear sweet Ursula, it is real! It is all real. The Root of a Thousand Eyes... all of it! The woods up here, they creak and groan. They are alive.

The captain made the sacrifice and was blessed with the Avatar of Sin. It came from the roots, crawling up from the earth. We called it up! Just thinking about it again has made my hands tremble. I wish you could have seen it, though I don't think you're ready. Buford wasn't ready. His end was swift but painful.

Captain Smith tried to give his eye so he could see the door, but he was not powerful enough. The witch can do it though. Her blood runs with the old magic, and surely she can see the door once we sacrifice her eye. Yet, someone must use the hand to open it. I have been tasked to carve the hand, and so I shall. Perhaps I can even be blessed to use it!

With the door open, the Root of a Thousand Eyes can claim this world, and we shall be Kings among men.

When the moon is full and the stars have aligned, we can open the door. Praise be to the Root of a Thousand Eyes. The Root sees. The Root Feels. The Root knows.

The witch's blood will lead us to the truth.

The rest of the book contained dozens of sketches of the wooden hand to include measurements, drawings of the strange sigils, and notes. Apparently, Jackson had tried several times and failed to create the hand. Evelyn only hoped he hadn't succeeded yet.

Mention of the witch ignited a fire underneath Evelyn's feet. She was sure Theresa was still alive, but for how much longer, she had no clue. The full moon was only a day or two away.

She had to get up to Summit Park and find Theresa before it was too late.

CHAPTER 8

Evelyn urged Stinker up the road. The sun was just starting to peek up above the mountains; Evelyn hoped it would bring warmth with its rays. Her breath formed small clouds in the crisp morning air, and it was hard to not start shivering.

During the night, the landscape had given way from sagebrush to a thick forest of aspen trees. They had just started to turn to their fall colors and painted the landscape with yellows and oranges. The leaves danced and shook in the slight breeze giving off the quiet rattle. Typically, Evelyn took comfort amongst such sights and sounds, but there was something... *off* with these trees. The knots in the wood looked too much like eyes watching her every move. But then, the snap of branches and limbs came from deep within the woods, and Evelyn couldn't help but recall Jackson's journal entry.

The woods up here, they creak and groan. They are alive.

Even Stinker, who was usually quite stoic even in the worst of situations, huffed and looked about with nervous anxiety. Evelyn gently patted Stinker's neck.

"It's okay. We'll be out of this soon enough. But I need you to be strong, got it?"

Stinker let out a whinny, but it lacked its usual bravado.

The aspens grew thicker, and Evelyn wondered how much labor it had taken to clear this patch of road. Through the talk and gossip, she had heard that it was an overzealous undertaking by Judge Carter and that he and his team had hit a lot of setbacks during its construction.

As they gained elevation, tall lodgepole pines mixed with the aspen trees, creating a beautiful display of colors. She came across a small creek running alongside the road and stopped to let Stinker have a drink. Evelyn dismounted Stinker and pulled the map out of her pocket, trying to determine how much further ahead it would be before they arrived at Summit Park.

According to the map, she surmised maybe another hour or so, but given it wasn't drawn to scale, it was hard to determine with any amount of accuracy. Hopefully, she would hear the sawmill long before she arrived so she could pick her avenue of approach.

"You about ready?" Evelyn asked.

Stinker looked up at her after taking another drink from the stream. Water dripped from his nose and mouth, and he shook his head to fling it off. Most of it landed on

Evelyn, causing her to squeal and cover her face with her arms.

"Thanks."

Stinker chuckled and took a bite from some grass. Evelyn wiped her face dry and then mounted up and headed back up the road.

Finally, the sun rose high enough to bathe her with its rays and shed the morning cold. Evelyn pulled some of the bread and dried meat from her pack and ate what little she could stomach, as her guts were twisted with worry. However, she knew that it would affect her judgment and reflexes if she didn't eat.

The road led up a hill and took a slight curve. As they turned the corner, three horses came into view. Mounted on two of them were soldiers. They wore second-hand uniforms without much care for professionalism. One man had his coat and shirt unbuttoned and a red beard that poked out in different directions.

The other didn't even have a hat and smoked a pipe. A lazy trail of smoke led from the pipe up into the air, and Evelyn caught the cloying scent of the tobacco from where she was.

The third had long, greasy black hair and stood by a nearby tree, pissing. Evelyn thought about turning around, but Red Beard saw her almost immediately. He smacked his smoking partner on the shoulder and pointed at her.

Evelyn cursed under her breath but kept riding forward, hoping these buffoons wouldn't bother her. However, she knew it was already too late for that. Maybe they would simply whistle and make inappropriate remarks.

"Hey there, Virgil, look at this," the smoking soldier said.

The man who was relieving himself turned his head and looked down the road directly at Evelyn and smiled, revealing a mouth with several missing teeth.

"Well, what do we have here?" Virgil asked.

He buttoned up his trousers and walked over to his horse.

"Looks like we have ourselves a lady all alone," Red Beard said. "Where's your husband at?"

Evelyn ignored the question and kept riding towards the group. "How much further to the sawmill at Summit Park?"

The three soldiers looked at each other and smiled. The smoking man took another puff on his pipe and leaned forward on his saddle.

"Now, what does a lady like you want up at the sawmill?" he asked.

By this time, Evelyn had ridden up next to them. Virgil walked alongside her, keeping pace with Stinker. Evelyn considered pushing past them but didn't want to show weakness to this group of hungover soldiers judging by the strong smell of whiskey.

"My associate asked you a question. What do you want with the sawmill, and what are you doing up here all alone?" Virgil asked, glancing back down the road again.

"That's Pinkerton business. Now answer my question."

"You hear that boys! Pinkerton business," Virgil said.

Red Beard let out a whistle, his eyes wide with feigned surprise. The other just chuckled and took another puff from his pipe.

"Ain't no women Pinkertons," Virgil said and grabbed Stinker's reins.

Red Beard spurred his horse forward and got in front of Evelyn. The other positioned himself on her flank, opposite Virgil. Evelyn did not like where this was going. She was almost completely surrounded.

"Let me pass, or I'll drag all three of you to the marshal down in Ashley for hindering my investigation," Evelyn said.

There was malicious glee in Virgil's eyes. The man quickly glanced away to his compatriots and scratched his head. "Well, she's older than we like, but beggars can't be choosers up on the mountain, can we boys?"

"Sure can't," the smoking soldier said.

Virgil reached up to grab Evelyn, but she was quicker. She drew her pistol and shoved the barrel into Virgil's mouth, knocking one of his few remaining teeth out. He howled in pain, though it was muffled with an inch of the pistol in his yapper. Evelyn grabbed the Colt Navy with her other hand and pointed it right at Red Beard. His hand was halfway to his gun. She didn't have a bead on the smoking man but hoped that he was just as shocked as the other two.

"Don't," Evelyn said. "You might get the drop on me. Maybe not. But one thing's for sure, regardless of whether you can, I'll blow your shit-for-brains friend's head clean off before your fingers ever touch your gun."

"She's lying. Kill her boys!" Virgil mumbled.

Evelyn kept her eyes locked on Red Beard but pulled the hammer back on the pistol in Virgil's mouth.

"You can certainly test that theory. However, I doubt you'll like the results."

Red Beard and Evelyn stared at one another. The man's eye twitched, and all the while, the Colt Navy whispered its sweet lies into Evelyn's ear.

Kill him. If you let them live, they'll just cause trouble later. Besides, I haven't eaten in such a long time. Kill him, and I can help you find your friend.

Evelyn shuddered and used sheer willpower to quiet the voice.

"I got places to be; now make your decision. Either go for that piece and let's light this candle, or let me pass," Evelyn said.

After a few more seconds that were more like an eternity, Red Beard moved his hand away from his weapon. Evelyn let out a deep breath and motioned for the others to move in front of her.

"Get to where I can see you and keep those hands up. If I even get a whiff that one of you is going to try something, I'll kill you all right here and now."

The smoking soldier urged his horse over to Red Beard's. He was still smoking, but his eyes promised pain. Virgil joined his friends and spat on the ground.

"You better keep your eyes peeled, bitch. Because one of these days we—"

"Strip," Evelyn said, cutting Virgil off.

"What?"

"Are you deaf as well as fucking stupid? I said strip. All of you! Get off those horses and out of those clothes."

"What are you going to do?" Red Beard asked.

"I'm going to shoot you in the knee if you don't get shed them clothes."

Virgil unbuttoned his shirt and started to undress. That set the other two into motion. Soon all three stood in the middle of the road covering their genitals. Evelyn gathered up their clothes and horses.

"You can't leave us here like this. We'll die," Virgil said.

"Maybe. Maybe not. If I ever see any of you again. I'll kill you without a second thought. You remember that. I reckon what I'm doing here is more of a kindness than any of you deserve. Now walk off this mountain and don't come back."

They all stared at each other for a bit, then finally, the trio started their trek down the road toward the bottom. Evelyn watched them go until they got out of sight, then holstered the Colt Navy. As soon as she did, a weight disappeared from her chest. She could breathe easier and a slight ringing in her ears she hadn't noticed before stopped.

Evelyn hated that pistol from the moment she had pulled it from the iron box buried at the Church of the Wayward Soul back in the slot canyons way to the south. At times, she wished she had never found it, but it had already proven its worth, and Evelyn surmised it would prove useful again. The legends said it could kill a god. Evelyn wasn't sure if that was true or not, but if that creature from Ursula's showed up again, she would certainly test that theory. It had made short work of some quite unnatural things so far.

Evelyn took off with the gear and horses in tow. After about ten minutes, she dumped the clothes into the woods, unsaddled the horses, and set them loose.

Evelyn directed Stinker back to the road. After another hour, the drone of saws on wood filled the air, telling her they were close. Yet, the trees seemed to watch her with renewed interest ever since that encounter with the three soldiers.

The weight of their gaze bore through her heart.

CHAPTER 9

Evelyn rode Stinker closer to the sawmill. Nearby, a few men prepared fallen trees for the mill by stripping down branches and arranging the timber nearby. The savory aroma of cooked bacon and coffee wafted through the air, causing Evelyn's stomach to grumble.

She realized it had been over a day since she'd had a proper meal and couldn't wait to get back to civilization where she could bathe, sleep in an actual bed, and eat some fine food. Unfortunately, luxuries such as that had started to occur further and further apart. Perhaps it was time to settle down and retire. But not until she had saved Theresa and dealt with Captain Smith.

Some men gave her strange looks as she rode through, but most didn't even give her any attention. They had a task to do, and she wasn't part of that task.

Evelyn rode up to a man who wore a ratty hat that looked older than the Union. He was an elderly gentleman with grey eyes and a weathered expression. However, there was warmth behind the patina.

"Good morning," Evelyn said, tipping her hat toward him.

"And a fine morning to you, ma'am. How can I help you?"

"I'm looking for someone who can answer some questions for me. I'm on official Pinkerton business."

The man nodded as if he knew what she was talking about. He pointed over to a canvas tent where a person stood next to a desk. He had his back to them.

"You'll want to speak to Emmett over there. He's in charge of this operation."

"Much obliged," Evelyn said. "Oh, one more thing if you don't mind?"

"Shoot."

"You seen or heard anything strange up here?"

The old timer's expression shifted. His smile dropped, and he looked away towards the tree. "Uh, no ma'am. I have to get back to work now."

"Of course, thank you."

Evelyn left him, wondering what he had seen that made him so nervous. Perhaps it was that same creature that attacked Ursula. Regardless, Evelyn decided not to push the matter and rode toward the tent. She dismounted Stinker and walked up to the tent's opening. Inside, she could see maps hanging off the walls with sections of the mountain marked for timber. The man at the desk still had his back to her and hadn't noticed Evelyn ride up.

"Excuse me, are you Emmett?" Evelyn asked.

"One moment, please," Emmett said and held his hand up. He made a few more notes, then turned toward her.

Emmett had greying black hair cut short and brown eyes that looked like they had seen a lot. He had a tight expression on his face, but it looked more like a man who wanted to get back to their duties than anger or irritation.

"How can I help you, ma'am?" Emmett asked.

"I'm Evelyn Horn, a Pinkerton. I'm here to meet with Captain Smith. Can you tell me where he is, please?"

Emmet's brows furrowed. "Well, Captain Smith would be back at the fort. I hope you didn't ride up here just to speak with him."

"That's odd. He asked me to come up here and speak with him regarding the matters of my investigation. He seemed very interested in hearing what I could dig up regarding certain... individuals."

It was a lie, but Evelyn banked on Emmett not catching on. If he did, things could turn ugly very fast, as there were way too many workers up at the sawmill for her to deal with.

"Well, maybe he came up last night and went straight to the cabin," Emmett said. "He doesn't tell me much about his comings or goings. I'm just here to work these trees."

"Can you tell me where the cabin is? He never mentioned it other than saying it was nearby the sawmill." Evelyn took a chance, digging the hole of her lie even deeper. She would either find gold or realize she dug her own grave.

Emmett walked over to one of the maps. Evelyn followed him in, wary of a trap. However, she trusted Emmett more than anyone else she had encountered so far. It was something about his eyes and the way he carried himself. Evelyn generally had good instincts about a person's character. It was a skill she'd had to hone early in life, especially with her chosen profession. Emmett was a decent person.

He pointed at a spot on the map. "We are here. If you follow the road back down a bit, you'll come to a point where the creek cuts through this saddle. The cabin isn't too far from this point. You'll have to cross at some point, but keep the creek on your left and follow the mountain."

Evelyn studied the map for a bit. She stepped back when she felt like she could remember it well enough. "Thank you."

"You're welcome. I've got a man out that way scouting for more good trees we can cut down. If you come across him and tell him I sent you, I'm sure he'll be more than happy to take a break and lead you to the cabin. You'll know him by the pheasant feather in his hatband."

"Thanks again. I really appreciate your help," Evelyn said.

"My pleasure."

Evelyn left Emmett in the tent and mounted Stinker. She rode out of the camp back toward the road. As she did, the old-timer stared at her, wearing a worried expression on his wrinkled face. He waved as she rode by.

The sound of saws and men talking faded as she left the sawmill behind. In a way, it was nice being around so many other people because Evelyn liked to think the creature wouldn't attack with a crowd around. However, she realized she knew next to nothing about the monster, and perhaps it wasn't afraid at all of people. Maybe it fed off of fear?

On the other hand, Evelyn thrived when she was in her own element. She had survived most of her fifty years on this earth on her own, and she knew she could rely on her abilities.

You are strong. You could be stronger.

Evelyn glanced down and found her palm resting on the Colt Navy. She snatched it away, feeling sick to her stomach.

Evelyn followed the creek like Emmett had instructed at one point. Finally, she came across a section that looked fine to cross and urged Stinker through the water so she could keep the creek on her left.

The smell of pine mixed with the clean air around the water was quite peaceful. This was a place Evelyn would have liked to spend time relaxing if it weren't for the threat of murderous tree creatures and devious Army captains. It was beautiful on the mountainside. Peaceful.

Eventually, Evelyn came to the saddle and continued onward. According to the map and Emmett's instructions, the cabin shouldn't be too much farther. The path cut up higher into the mountains a ways. Soon, the trees grew thicker, and the scenery turned from being peaceful to being ominous. The birds and squirrels had gone quiet, and Evelyn couldn't shake the feeling that something watched her.

Evelyn slowed Stinker down so she could better hear what was going on around her. It didn't take long before the snap of a twig came from behind them. Somebody, or something, was following.

Evelyn stopped Stinker and turned him around. At the same time, she placed her hand on the Colt Navy in the saddle. If it was the creature again, this time she would be prepared and it wouldn't get away.

A cold shock traveled up her fingertips and along her arm as soon as she touched the pistol's grip. It made her ears ring, and for a second, her vision blurred. When it cleared, a man stood before her on the path. He had an ax on his shoulder, a brown shirt, black trousers, and a wide-brimmed hat with a pheasant feather sticking from the hatband.

It was Emmett's timber scout.

It also happened to be Billy "the Cannibal" Hughes.

CHAPTER 10

The man that stood in the woods in front of Evelyn had to be Billy. He had the same lazy eye and gap-toothed grin from the wanted poster she kept tucked away in her saddle bag.

"You lost?" Billy asked.

Evelyn wanted to jerk her pistol and take him back to Ashley so she could hand him off to a federal marshal and be done with that chapter of her life. Billy had murdered his way across the continent, leaving a trail of half-eaten corpses in his wake. He had eaten the daughter of a rich man in Pennsylvania, which is how the Pinkertons got involved in the first place. However, Evelyn didn't want to think just how many poor souls had fallen victim to his ravenous desires.

Evelyn had been looking for Billy ever since she received notice from Pinkerton headquarters nearly seven months ago.

However, it appeared that he had no idea who Evelyn was or that she was looking for him. Billy could wait, as Theresa was the most important matter.

"Might be. I'm looking for Captain Smith's cabin. Emmett, back at the sawmill, said you could lead me there. He mentioned you had a pheasant feather in your hat." Evelyn pointed to the long tailfeather with alternating black and brown patches along its length.

Billy ran a finger across the feather. He stared at Evelyn for a few seconds before nodding.

"Sure. Follow me. It isn't too far from here."

Billy turned and trudged up the hill. Evelyn couldn't believe the turn of events! She wracked her brain trying to figure out a way that she could save Theresa, end Captain Smith, and bring Billy back for trial and justice. Although, if worse came to absolute worst, Evelyn had no qualms putting a bullet in his brain and bringing him back dead. The wanted posters did say dead or alive.

The big question on Evelyn's mind was why Billy was up here to begin with? Was he helping Captain Smith, or was he trying to earn a little money before moving along?

"So, I didn't catch your name," Evelyn said.

"I didn't give it."

"Right, how long have you been working on the mountain?"

"Not long," Billy said. "Hey, have you eaten breakfast yet?"

Evelyn didn't like where this was going. "No, I haven't."

"Me neither. I'm so hungry. Hopefully, they'll have something ready at the cabin. I left the sawmill early this morning before breakfast was ready. They had some biscuits, but I'm more of a meat person, you know what I mean?"

Evelyn's hand wandered towards the Colt Navy on its own. Her fingertips brushed across the cold grip causing her breath to catch.

Destroy this monster. How many people... how many children has he consumed?

How many indeed? Evelyn knew the official body count for Billy was twelve, which included three children. However, she was sure there had to be more they didn't know about. Nobody would balk at her killing him. He was a monster, and monsters were meant to be killed.

Evelyn snatched her hand away from the pistol as if it were a viper. Then, the whispers faded, leaving her wondering if they had been real.

Up ahead, the cabin came into view. It was a ramshackle hut, put together with unfinished timber and sitting at a slant. However, smoke wafted from the chimney, and several horses were hitched outside. Some of the horses bore military brandings and gear.

Billy stopped and turned to look Evelyn in the eyes. "Looks like the captain is there. Good fire going too. I wonder if they are preparing my special meal. One they promised me," Billy said. As he finished the thought, his lips curled into a cruel smile.

Billy must have seen through her façade.

Evelyn hoped she could have avoided this, especially so close to the cabin. However, there wasn't any other choice. She yanked her pistol from the holster and pointed it at him. "Billy Hughes, you are coming with me to face trial for your crimes."

The smile never faded from his face. "And what crimes are those?"

"Murder, evading the law, and cannibalism."

Billy placed the head of his ax on the ground and let the handle lean against his leg before taking his hat off. His hair was a greasy, thinning tangle.

"Have you ever consumed human flesh?"

"Shut yer mouth," Evelyn ordered. She tried to figure out what to do with the man and the others in the cabin.

"From a young age, I was curious. I'd eaten so many different types of God's creatures, but one always eluded me... made me curious. You see, it used to speak to me—human meat. I could hear it in my sleep, calling to me. The promise of power, ecstasy... oh and the taste."

Billy put his hat back on and kissed the tips of his fingers.

"Shut yer mouth now, or I'll shut it for you."

"The taste is divine. I know the gods devour humans, but now I know why. Sometimes the meat still whispers to me after I've taken it inside me."

"Enough! Answer me this, you sack of turkey shit. Is Theresa in there?"

A wicked gleam hit Billy's eyes. "The witch? She was very tender. And the secrets I discovered in her meat...."

Evelyn gritted her teeth so hard she thought they might break. She pulled the hammer back on her pistol, intent on sending Billy to the other side to face whatever demons and punishment he had earned, consequences be damned. Evelyn even contemplated using the Colt Navy and shredding the man's very existence into nothingness.

A low rumble, almost like a growl, emanated from the trees to her side. It almost sounded like a bear, but it was *off—deeper*, wet, and phlegmy. Evelyn glanced in the direction, but all she saw were trees. Though they seemed to stare at her. And were they closer than before?

Evelyn turned back to Billy just in time to see him hit her in the face with the ax handle.

CHAPTER 11

E velyn found herself in the dark, surrounded by aspen trees. Their leaves quaked in the wind, but there was something else behind the chitter—whispers.

Do you seek the truth?

Do you hear the creak and groan, the snap and crack of branch and bone?

Evelyn turned and found Raymond sitting on a nearby log next to a fire with black flames. He had his back to her, but she could pick Raymond out in a crowd with no trouble. There was a way he sat with his shoulders hunched and his head down that was uniquely Raymond.

It hurt to see him again, like pulling a scab off a nearly healed wound and starting the whole process over again. Only, this process had been going on for over twenty years now.

"Eve, the time is getting closer, you know."

Evelyn started to say something, but the words caught in her throat. She walked over next to the fire and sat down, though she couldn't bring herself to look at Raymond's face. If it wasn't his face and instead was that imposter, she didn't think she could take it again.

"Soon, you'll be with me in the dark. In the shadows where the old things writhe. Where you can find the truth."

His voice cracked, and for a moment, dozens of other voices joined in a chorus of damned souls, all saying the word, truth.

A light shined behind her.

"Evelyn?"

It was Theresa's voice.

Evelyn turned toward the light and found it too bright. She slammed her eyes shut and looked away. The rattle of chains clinked into her ears, causing her head to ache. Evelyn opened her eyes slowly, letting them adjust to the light, and found herself not in the woods but in a room. It was almost entirely dark save for a sliver of sunlight that came through a hole in the wall.

When she tried to move, she found her hands tied with rough-hewn rope and her leg secured with chain to a giant hook spiked into the wall.

"Is that really you, or is it a trick again?" Theresa asked.

Evelyn followed Theresa's voice and found her similarly bound and chained. Her breath caught in her throat when Theresa moved into the sun's rays, revealing a bloody bandage over one eye. Her hair was tangled, dirty, and knotted, and her other eye was swollen.

Evelyn moved closer to Theresa, and they shared an awkward embrace made almost impossible by their bonds.

"Oh my god, I thought you were dead," Evelyn said.

Tears welled up in her eyes, rolling down her cheeks and onto the dirt floor.

"What are you doing here?" Theresa asked.

"Looking for you. I came to the fort looking for a murderer and somehow stumbled into all of this. I'm just happy you're alive."

"I'm happy to see you, but you shouldn't have come. Not this time," Theresa said, sitting up straight. "We're in too deep this time, and I don't think there's a damn thing either one of us can do to get out of this situation."

"We have to try and stay positive. I think we can get out of here."

More movement caught Evelyn's attention, and she found five others were in the room with them. Three men and two women. A couple of the men wore army uniforms—they were each gagged with a dirty cloth. The others didn't dare make eye contact with Evelyn or Theresa.

"Who are they?" Evelyn asked.

"Sacrifices."

"For the ritual... What happened to you?"

Theresa sighed. "That disgusting human being, Captain Smith, caught wind that I was a witch. He came to pay me a visit, and I knew right away he was bad business. He asked me a few questions, but the way he moved and his aura was all wrong... He made my skin crawl. I was trying to figure out what was going on, doing my own investigation like you, and he returned five days later with some of his goons. Long story short, here I am."

"And the eye?" Evelyn asked, already surmising the answer.

"Captain Smith cut it out. He said I would be the eye that could see the door."

Theresa started to cry, and the waterworks started anew with Evelyn. She let Theresa lay her head on her shoulder and did her best to comfort the woman.

"It's okay. We're going to get out of this. I'll make that sonofabitch pay for what he did to you. Mark my words."

"I wish they had killed me," Theresa said.

"Don't say that."

"No! I'm afraid when they use me for this blasted ritual, I won't be able to stop it."

"It's okay. It's okay... We just won't let him start it then."

Theresa started crying harder. "Why did you have to come? Why?"

"I couldn't stay behind knowing you might be up here in danger," Evelyn said.

Theresa looked Evelyn in the eyes. "I've seen it."

"Seen what?"

"I've seen your death," Theresa said.

Evelyn already knew what was coming.

"You will die in shadow, surrounded by hate. The sky will weep, and the moon will be ripped from the night." As Theresa spoke, her voice held the same pitch and tone as the sorceress Evelyn had shot down in Fairfield many years ago.

"None of us know what's coming," Evelyn said. Though that was a lie. Evelyn had stared into the darkness enough times to see what was on the other side. She had even stepped into the land of death long ago, only to be ripped back to the mortal plane by Theresa's willpower alone. Evelyn didn't look forward to the afterlife, not if it meant going to the same place Raymond was. A place of lies and shadow... truth be damned.

That day back in Fairfield had started Evelyn down a new path of cosmic dread and truths that were better left unknown. However, that path also let Evelyn know Theresa, and she would never give that up in a million years.

"We're going to get out of this. You trust me, don't you?" Evelyn asked.

Theresa nodded.

"Do you remember that wooden hand you took when we parted ways?"

"Yes," Theresa said.

"The captain didn't take it, did he?"

"No."

Relief flooded Evelyn. Without the hand, they couldn't open the door.

"But it doesn't matter," Theresa said. "They've carved a new one. I've seen it, and it's exactly the same."

"Damnit."

Before she could say anything else, the door opened. A man with a lantern walked in, and the extra light hurt Evelyn's eyes, causing her to shy away. The others in the room groaned as well.

Heavy footsteps in the dirt came toward Evelyn. She slowly opened her eyes and found Captain Smith crouched next to her, holding the lantern up so he could better see her face.

"Miss Horn," Captain Smith said with a sigh. "You couldn't just leave well enough alone, could you?"

"You best let us all go right now," Evelyn said.

"You're hardly in any position to make demands. If you had minded your own business, you could have lived out the rest of your days in peace. But now, well, now you get to take part in the shaping of history."

"Many men have sought to shape history. Most of them die lonely and forgotten."

The captain smiled. "We'll see then, won't we?"

He stood and walked back to the doorway.

"You know the Pinkertons will send more detectives to find me when I don't check in, don't you?"

"It won't matter," Captain Smith said. "After tonight, they could send the entire army, and it wouldn't make a difference."

He walked out the door, and soldiers filed in. One by one, they unchained the prisoners and led them all outside. Once outside, the soldiers tethered the prisoners together with rope before securing the other end to one of the horses. Evelyn saw Stinker. A portly soldier with a thin blonde beard had Stinker's reins in one hand. Her Colt Navy was still in the holster.

Next to him was Jackson Francis. Evelyn recognized the man from Ursula's picture. He sat on the back of a sizeable black workhorse that was more suited to plowing than traipsing through the forest. He stared back at Evelyn with calculating eyes.

Captain Smith mounted his horse. "Let's get moving. We have a ways to go before we get to the site."

Before they could leave, Emmett rode over on a dapple grey mare. When he saw the prisoners, his face scrunched up in confusion.

"What is this?" he asked.

Captain Smith turned his horse around and rode next to Emmett. "This is army business. I suggest you head on back to the sawmill and let me and my men deal with this."

"What kind of army business. That's Theresa Huntington. She's no criminal. She helped me through a bad bout of pneumonia two winters ago. I'd be dead if it weren't for her," Emmett said.

"It's always the ones you least expect. I'm sorry to be the bearer of bad news, but I am not allowed to get into the details. Now move along."

The procession started, leaving Emmett behind, watching them go. Evelyn nodded to him as she walked by, but Emmett didn't say or do anything, though his eyes were full of conflict.

Billy Hughes walked up next to Evelyn, still packing the ax on his shoulder.

"Maybe I'll get that special meal after all," he said. Billy sniffed Evelyn's neck, and she shouldered him away.

Billy laughed as they walked through the forest. The sound bounced off the trees and made it sound like they were the ones laughing.

Maybe they were.

CHAPTER 12

They walked for hours through the mountains, passing by small ponds and wallows, even spooking a herd of elk that had bedded in some tall grass next to an open meadow. Evelyn watched them go, the lead cow turning to look at the intruders with worry before following the rest of the elk and disappearing into the timber.

Evelyn eyed Stinker, who was nearby. Billy had long since mounted him and rode her horse as they trudged through the trees. When Billy saw Evelyn looking at him, he gave her a smile and winked.

"You know, I haven't eaten horse, but I'm not opposed to trying it out," he said.

Evelyn didn't give him the satisfaction of a response. Instead, she looked away from him and at the Colt Navy holstered on the saddle. She imagined the bullet from that weapon ripping his soul out and blasting it into shreds.

"What is that?" Theresa asked.

"That is an affront to reality," Evelyn said. "It's rumored to be able to kill anything on this earth. Perhaps even an ancient tree god."

"That weapon can only bring pain and sadness," Theresa said. "I can feel its pull from here. Where did you get it?"

Evelyn shuddered as her mind involuntarily went back to that fateful night. Back to that abandoned church in a town that shouldn't have been there.

"If we get out of this, I'll tell you about it," she said.

"You should throw that pistol in a lake and let it sink to the bottom."

"Maybe," Evelyn said. "But it's too valuable to lose right now. Besides, we need it."

"There is always another way."

Evelyn turned to look Theresa in the eyes. "That's what I love about you. Always the optimist."

Theresa's cheeks glowed red, and she looked away. "Somebody has to try and battle the pessimism in you."

"Enough chatter. Shut your mouths, or I'll gag the both of you," Captain Smith said as he rode by.

They continued the forced march, eventually coming to a drainage rut leading down the mountain. After an initial rocky descent that took longer than Captain Smith would have liked—given how much he started swearing—the path eventually smoothed out. The pines gave way to more aspen, and Evelyn couldn't help but feel their gaze upon her as they continued their trek. There were whispers in their leaves, promising dark things.

The sun had begun to set, but it was still light enough to see, though not too far. Something moved in the trees, just out of sight, but it had enough size that branches and smaller saplings snapped as it moved through. She couldn't see it, but she sure as hell could feel it. It was a strange sensation that made her skin crawl.

"What is that?" Evelyn asked.

"It is the Avatar of Sin, the Harbinger of Truth," Theresa said, staring out into the aspens. "It has come to ensure the ritual occurs and the sacrifices are offered to the Root of a Thousand Eyes."

As if in response, the creature growled, filling the dusky air with its trill scream. Some of the prisoners started to panic, but Captain Smith and the other soldiers got them back into marching order.

"Not much farther," Smith said.

The last part of the trail was steep, and Evelyn slipped on a loose rock, falling to the ground. Theresa and an elderly gentleman tethered to Evelyn's other side helped her back up.

"Thank you," Evelyn said.

The old man nodded, but his eyes were full of defeat. Evelyn had seen that look before on many others. It was a look that said they had given up hope.

"Don't worry, I will get us out of this mess," Evelyn said to the old man.

He nodded, but his look told her he didn't take much stock in her words. Hell, Evelyn had a hard time believing in herself at the moment.

Eventually, the path leveled out, revealing a picturesque meadow. Aspens and pines surrounded all sides of the field, and a small stream cut through the middle. It was really quite breathtaking, or would have been if it weren't for the dozens of mutilated sheep.

They lay across the landscape, white puffy balls of blood and gore. As the group neared the first one, Evelyn suppressed her shock when she saw tiny aspens growing up through the corpse. Then, to her horror, the sheep let out a quiet mew.

It was still alive.

They were all still alive.

The sheep began to scream and cry, filling the meadow with a cacophony of pain and fear. Theresa covered her ears and dropped to her knees. The elderly gentleman behind Evelyn threw up before curling into a ball on the ground. Even the soldiers looked nervous, clutching their weapons and looking all around for anything they could attack to make it all stop.

From the tree line came another screaming growl from the Avatar of Sin, and at once, the sheep went silent and stopped moving.

For a long while, nothing happened. Nobody moved or dared to breathe. Then, finally, Captain Smith turned his horse around to face the others.

"Get a bonfire going in the middle of this meadow. Make it big."

The men nodded and rode off to get started.

"You two, secure the prisoners over there. Billy, take care of the horses," Smith said. "We have a lot to do and not much time. It will be the full moon tonight, and we have one shot at this."

That gave Evelyn one shot to sabotage the ritual.

CHAPTER 13

Evelyn sat on the ground, still trying to figure a way out of her bonds without anyone seeing. The soldiers had followed Captain Smith's orders and created a huge bonfire that lit up the night sky. The flames reached high into the air, taller than a house, and even from where Evelyn sat, the fire bathed her skin with its warmth.

Captain Smith strolled by with the ritual papers in his hands. He stopped next to Evelyn.

"You know, you're kind of a blessing in disguise. When my soldiers never returned from the witch's cabin, I figured the instructions were lost. But by the luck of the roots, here they are, hand-delivered by you."

Evelyn didn't reply; instead, she stared daggers at him and imagined different ways to kill the man. He smiled as he walked away. A moment later, Billy came slinking from the shadows. He poked a stick at one of the women.

"I'm going to eat you first. You look delicious. I bet your thigh cooks up nice and juicy."

The woman shied away from him.

"Leave her alone," Evelyn said.

Billy looked at Evelyn, the firelight reflected in his eyes. He crawled over to her, but Evelyn did her best not to flinch away.

"I'll probably make you into a stew. I bet you're stringy."

"I hope you choke to death on one of my bones," Evelyn said.

Billy laughed and walked away. Evelyn decided right then and there she would bring him back dead.

The soldiers finished preparing the field around the bonfire. They had cleared out seven different spots according to Captain Smith's instructions.

Time was running out. However, when Jackson walked by with a small carved box in his hands, Evelyn got an idea.

"You know Ursula died horribly when the Avatar of Sin came for her," Evelyn said.

Jackson stopped and stared at her. At first, worry and anguish washed over his face, then doubt. "You're lying."

"I wish I was. I watched it all happen. All she wanted was for you to come back from all of this nonsense. But, instead, she paid the ultimate price for your actions."

Jackson sneered at her and then stormed over to Captain Smith.

"You said she would be protected! Now she's dead!" Jackson yelled.

Captain Smith stuffed the papers away in his coat and put an arm around Jackson. He tried to calm the man down, talking quietly.

"No! Promises were made, and now she's dead," Jackson said, pushing the captain away.

Smith walked back over to Jackson and led him further away, far enough that Evelyn couldn't hear them. The soldier standing guard over them turned away and walked closer to the Captain and Jackson so he could listen to the argument.

This was Evelyn's chance. She reached up to grab her hairpin dagger, yanking it free. Her hair cascaded down onto her shoulders. Evelyn's fingers had gone numb from the binds, and the dagger slipped free from her grasp and landed in the grass behind her.

"Damn it all to hell," Evelyn mumbled.

She felt around for the dagger but couldn't find where it had fallen. The mounting frustration and the fact that Captain Smith walked toward them with a newfound purpose and scowl upon his face made Evelyn even more desperate to find the knife.

However, it was too late. Captain Smith walked up and grabbed Theresa by the arm, pulling her to her feet.

"It's time," he said.

Theresa kicked and fought back, but she was bound, tired, and weak from the travel—she was no match for him. Evelyn continued to grab for the dagger but couldn't find it with her fingers.

"Let her go!" Evelyn said.

Captain Smith ignored Evelyn and dragged Theresa to the meadow, close to the bonfire. He shoved the papers into her hands.

"Begin the ritual," he said.

Theresa threw the papers down and spat on the captain. He growled before he slapped her with a quick backhand that knocked her to the ground. Captain Smith gathered the papers and thrust them back into Theresa's hands.

"Do it now."

"Go to hell," Theresa said.

All the while, Evelyn scrambled to try and find the dagger, but she couldn't. She couldn't pull her eyes away from Theresa, afraid that something horrible would happen if she did, though she couldn't quite explain it. The woods themselves watched it all unfold with anticipation.

Captain Smith pulled his revolver from his hip holster and first pointed it at Theresa but then moved it to Evelyn.

"Read the papers, or I will kill your dear friend in front of you."

Theresa stared at Evelyn, and even though they were far apart and no words were spoken, none were needed. Evelyn knew that Theresa would read the papers regardless of the greater good. The look of anguish on Theresa's face hurt more than any gunshot wound.

Evelyn shook her head and mouthed the word *don't*. She tried to convey that feeling with all of her willpower and intent; however, she knew it was futile. Theresa was going to do it. Evelyn knew because she would do the same in her position.

"I'm sorry," Theresa said.

Theresa looked down at the papers, cleared her throat, and said the first word. It sounded like a crack of thunder that rumbled through the skies. The ground beneath Evelyn trembled with excitement, and the aspens began to shake and quiver.

Evelyn's heart crawled into her throat as the very atmosphere around her began to change. There was a charge in the air that crept across her skin. The other prisoners whimpered, shuffling around nervously as they awaited what would happen next. Even the horses tamped the ground with their hooves and pulled against their reins.

Captain Smith smiled. "Continue."

Theresa began to read in earnest. The words ripped through her vocal cords with their alien intonations. However, if Theresa didn't know how to pronounce them, it didn't show. She read the passages as if they were her native tongue. Evelyn knew it to be true, deep down in the primal parts of her brain as if the knowledge had been there all along, locked away in her subconscious.

The words dripped with power.

Evelyn felt sick to her stomach but kept her bile down. Unfortunately, most of the other prisoners weren't so lucky, and some had evacuated their bowels and bladders judging from the smell.

Theresa's voice rose in a crescendo, and as it did, the bonfire burned low, falling to nothing but a smoldering pile of ash. The woods went silent, and the only sound was Theresa's voice and the pitiful moans of the prisoners behind Evelyn. Some soldiers began to back away, but Captain Smith stood his ground.

Theresa's voice took on a deep timbre. Her body convulsed, shaking violently. She dropped the papers, but it didn't matter; the words continued to spew forth from her mouth. With one hand, she reached up and ripped the bloody bandage away from her face, revealing a dark pit where her eye used to be.

Evelyn watched in horror as a pinpoint of azure light formed in that socket. Then black smoke billowed out from her skull, splitting into seven different streams which arced high into the air before crashing back into the earth around the bonfire.

Captain Smith holstered his pistol before drawing a large Bowie knife from his boot. He severed his hand with inhuman strength with one fell slash, dropping to his knees and screaming in pain.

CHAPTER 14

Evelyn's heart dropped into her stomach as it all happened. She was too late, unable to stop Captain Smith... unable to save Theresa. Captain Smith stopped screaming. It took a few deep breaths, but soon he joined Theresa's chanting. As he did, Jackson walked over with the wooden box, opened the lid, and produced the carved hand.

Captain Smith took the carved hand and placed it on his bloody stump. The sigils and markings lit up with the same azure color as Theresa's eye. Perhaps it was the low light and all the smoke, but Evelyn swore one of the fingers on the hand twitched. The captain let out a laugh.

"It's working! Look, it's wo—" his words were cut off by a growl of pain. He held his stump up high and watched with wide eyes as roots grew from the carving, burrowing deep into his flesh and bone.

Captain Smith dropped to the ground, writhing in pain as the hand attached itself to him, but somehow his screams matched the tone of Theresa's incantations, adding to them in some horrible chorus.

The sheep lying on the ground began to bleat, though somehow behind their cries were the wails of people. Evelyn thought she could hear Raymond's voice amongst the chaos. She curled into the fetal position and covered her ears, but it did little to quiet the din.

The bonfire flared to life once again, burning blue. Something in that fire tugged at Evelyn's soul, and for a moment, she wanted nothing more than to walk into the flames and offer herself to the fiery oblivion.

But it wasn't oblivion. Instead, it was a star burning bright somewhere in the vastness and deadly cold of space. How Evelyn knew this, she could not fathom, but she did know it deep down in her heart. That star was the Root of a Thousand Eyes, and it peered through her as if she were nothing more than a drop of rain.

One of the soldiers couldn't help himself. He stumbled forward, pulled along like a fish on a hook, and walked straight into the cerulean fire. He screamed as the flame touched his flesh, though that scream became distorted as he was sucked into the fire. It started with his outstretched hand, the skin literally pulling free from the bone and flowing into inferno like liquid. The tendons liquified and followed suit, then the bones of his fingers. Evelyn watched in horror as he came apart piece by piece and entered the blaze until he was no more.

The bonfire grew hotter after it had consumed the soldier, and the pull strengthened. Captain Smith stood and laughed. His laughter was deep and old, for he was no longer Captain Smith but something else. Something... other.

He turned to Billy and gave the man a wicked, inhuman smile. "You will be the first."

His voice creaked and cracked like a tree bending in high winds when he spoke. Billy's face turned from horror to shock.

"Me? What...? We had a deal!" Billy said, taking a step backward.

"Did you really believe a wretch like you would be given such an honor?" Captain Smith said.

"You can't!"

Two soldiers rushed over and dragged Billy to the first spot near the bonfire. He continued to fight and kick, managing to break away from one of them. He punched the other, laying the man out in the grass, clutching a broken nose. Billy turned to run but ran into Captain Smith, who stood next to him.

Smith grabbed Billy by the throat and lifted him into the air with one arm. He made it look easy as if Billy were nothing more than a sack full of apples. Billy grabbed at the captain's arm, hitting and kicking, but it was to no avail.

Captain Smith brought his other hand, the one with the wooden carving, up to Billy's chest.

"Your blood will feed the roots, and they shall grow. Your heart will beat for the Root of a Thousand Eyes."

Billy tried to say something, but the captain was choking him, and Billy's words came out as a garbled gasp. The captain flexed his arm, and the fingers of the wooden hand turned into large thorns that glistened in the firelight that slowly dug into Billy's chest.

Billy screamed as he tried to wriggle away. The finger spikes drove through his chest, finally protruding out his back.

Captain Smith withdrew his hand, ripping Billy's still-beating heart out of his body. He dropped Billy to the ground and held the heart up into the air, chanting in that strange language that hurt Evelyn's very being.

The ground shook, and a bloody aspen tree burst forth from the dirt, spiraling up into the night sky. Two small branches grew out, creating a holding place in which Captain Smith placed Billy's heart. The branches wrapped around the offering, and the aspen sprouted blood-red leaves that quivered erratically.

In the distance, something big moved amongst the trees. They cracked and snapped as it moved closer and closer to the circle and flame. Captain Smith turned to one of the soldiers, a portly fellow whose face had blanched whiter than fresh snow.

"Bring me another and put them there," the Captain said and pointed to the spot next to Billy's twitching corpse.

Although Billy should have been dead, his mouth opened and closed as he continued to make a strange mewling sound, much like a sheep. It was as if the peculiar aspen was keeping his body functioning.

Evelyn wondered if he was still conscious through some dark magic or force of the cosmos. She hoped not, as that had many implications.

Theresa, still chanting, moved away from Billy and almost danced over to the next spot where the soldier had deposited one of the prisoners. It was the old woman. Tears ran down her face, but she stood tall.

"You'll burn in hell for what you've wrought, Captain Smith," the old woman said.

He walked over to her and reached out to caress her cheek with the wooden hand. The woman shied away from his touch but spit on his uniform.

"Continue the ritual," Captain Smith said.

Theresa began to chant louder, her body swaying back and forth to a rhythm that was only in her head. Evelyn watched in horror as the smoke from her skull swirled around the old woman.

At first, there was nothing, but then the woman screamed. A root burst from the ground, impaling her through the abdomen. Her screams became choked as the root twisted up and re-impaled itself through her chest, tearing away flesh, muscle, and bone to expose her heart to the open air.

Evelyn was in shock, unable to move or act as she witnessed the horrible atrocity that unfolded before her eyes. The soldiers brought the prisoners to the designated spots around the bonfire, and one by one, Theresa and the captain sacrificed them. Soon, their bodies stood as macabre scarecrows lining the fire, their hearts torn out and waiting.

A cold hand wrapped around Evelyn's mouth from behind, snapping her out of her stunned state.

It was her turn.

CHAPTER 15

Evelyn pulled away from the hands and spun around. It wasn't a guard waiting to take her for sacrifice, much to her surprise. It was Emmett. He held a finger up to his mouth and then pulled a knife from his belt.

The blade made quick work to her bonds, and once again, she was free. Emmett handed her a pistol.

"Why are you doing this?" Evelyn asked.

"This..." Emmett let his words die, and he looked to the bonfire, his eyes wide with fear. "This isn't right." Then stood tall, his ax on his shoulder. "Captain Smith!"

The captain turned and stared at Emmett. His lips twisted into a sneer. Emmett took one step and lifted the ax up and over his head before flinging it end-over-end at the captain. It spun toward the captain before burying itself in his chest and knocking him to the ground.

Emmett pulled a pistol and shot one of the guards, who raised a rifle in his direction. Another came from around a tree, and Evelyn took aim and shot the man in the face, dropping him in his tracks.

Evelyn didn't waste any more time. She sprinted over to Theresa, who still swayed next to the fire, repeatedly chanting in a language Evelyn couldn't fathom.

"Come on now, we got to get!" Evelyn said, her southern accent breaking through.

If Theresa could hear her or understand, she didn't let on. Evelyn shook her friend hard, but it didn't do anything.

A shot rang out, the bullet hitting one of the sacrificed prisoners in the arm next to Evelyn. Evelyn twisted toward the shot and raised her pistol, squeezing the trigger at the same time and dropping another guard in a smooth action.

"Come on! Snap out of it!" Evelyn said and slapped Theresa.

Despite the effort, Theresa ignored Evelyn and continued to chant. The rest of the guards turned tail and ran into the forest back up the path Evelyn and the others had traversed coming down. Even Jackson slinked away into the shadows as soon as Captain Smith went down.

Emmett walked over to Evelyn, staring out into the forest. He gripped his pistol so tight his knuckles turned white. He raised the gun, aiming at something in the trees, but lowered it again.

"We need to go," he said.

"Not without her."

Emmett holstered his pistol. "Fine, I'll carry her, but we need to go, now. There's something out there, I can fee—"

He ate his last words and looked at his chest in confusion. Evelyn followed his gaze and gasped. A spiky branch protruded from his body and blood oozed out of the wound, staining his shirt.

Captain Smith sat up and pulled the ax from his chest, flinging it away into the darkness. He had his wooden hand pointed at Emmett. The spiky branch in Emmett was actually one of Smith's elongated fingers. Another finger shot forward in the blink of an eye, lancing Emmett a second time.

The captain's fingers shot back toward his hand, returning to their normal length. Emmett dropped to the ground, clutching his chest. He looked up at Evelyn and coughed up a gout of blood.

He tried to stand, but the captain was already on his feet. He pointed his hand at Emmett again, and all of his fingers sprung forth, stabbing through Emmett's body at various points. The wooden spikes acted like vines this time, snaking around Emmett's body and again burrowing into different spots. Emmett moaned in pain.

Evelyn emptied the pistol into Captain Smith, but it didn't even distract him. She flung the weapon away and spied Stinker over by the horses.

Evelyn needed the Colt Navy.

"Come on!" Evelyn said and dragged Theresa along with her.

Theresa didn't fight back, but she didn't exactly help either, which made moving her difficult. Evelyn continued to muscle her along but stopped when she noticed the skin around Theresa's eyes begin to wrinkle. Her hair lost its natural luster, turning strawberry blonde to grey. Theresa was aging before Evelyn's very eyes.

Evelyn realized she couldn't take Theresa away from the ritual. Doing so would kill her.

She screamed into the night sky in frustration. "Come on, please! Snap out of it, I need you with me, okay?"

Theresa didn't respond. She continued to sway and chant as the smoke oozed out of her eye socket.

Captain Smith raised his hand and pulled Emmett close to him. Emmett screamed, trying to fight back, but the finger-vines had wrapped themselves around him securely.

The captain reeled him close before bringing him to eye level. "I bet you wish you had stayed at the sawmill now, don't you?"

Captain Smith's grimace turned into a smile, and Emmett's screams got louder. A wet, ripping noise followed by the snap of bone that sounded too much like breaking branches hit Evelyn's ears. The vines pulled in opposite directions and ripped Emmett's body in half, raining blood, viscera, and intestines onto the grassy ground below him.

Evelyn let Theresa go and rushed over to Stinker. Stinker let out a worried huff and pulled against the reins, trying to get away from Captain Smith. Evelyn snatched the Colt Navy from the saddle. Generally, she fought against its influence, but this time she almost smiled as the cold wormed its way up her arm. Her doubts and fears fled from her mind when she tightened her fingers around the grip of the blasted weapon.

Good. Now let me devour it.

Evelyn knew without a doubt that the pistol could kill the captain. She spun around and brought the gun up, only to find Captain Smith wasn't there anymore. Evelyn turned and saw him standing nearby. Before she could shoot, he pointed a finger at her.

Evelyn wasn't quick enough to dodge, and the finger hit her shoulder. It felt like an arrow piercing her as pain exploded throughout her arm.

She screamed in agony, losing grip on the pistol and letting it fall to the ground. The captain flung Evelyn's body back toward the bonfire, and the air was blasted from her lungs when she hit.

She tried to scream but couldn't form the sound. Evelyn rolled onto her back and looked up into the night sky as she tried to pull oxygen into her lungs. The stars danced and swirled before her eyes, forming patterns that burned into her psyche.

When she could breathe again, Evelyn got to her feet. The world swayed underneath her as her vision blurred. Evelyn wiped at her eyes, and eventually, she could see clearly.

Captain Smith stood in front of her.

Before Evelyn could react, the captain hit her with a backhand stronger than a horse's kick. It sent her flying backward. Evelyn hit the ground hard, and everything went black.

When she came to, Evelyn found herself lying on her side. This time it didn't hurt, but there was a strange taste in her mouth. She was fairly sure she had lost some teeth and possibly broke her jaw.

"They were wrong, you know?" Captain Smith said. "That creature? It isn't the Avatar of Sin. No, it is a beautiful manifestation of the Root's will, but it is no Avatar."

Evelyn sat up and fought the urge to vomit. From behind the captain, the trees parted, revealing the monster. It lumbered out into the open meadow close to the bonfire.

The creature's body was covered with scars she hadn't seen before. Yet they weren't just scars. They were more than that. They were symbols. Spirals with antlers on top of them, strange shapes and figures that undulated and made Evelyn's nose bleed.

The thing stood behind the captain and laid its claws on the man's shoulder.

"It isn't the Avatar. I am," Captain Smith said.

The creature's eyes glowed first yellow, then shifted into blue to match the flames of the fire. It tightened its grip on Captain Smith's shoulders, talons digging into skin and ripping it apart as if Smith was made of paper. Theresa chanted louder, dancing around the pair as the smoke trailed her.

Branches and vines burst from the creature's body and ripped into Captain Smith. Evelyn watched as the thing lifted Smith into the air and then up into its torso. The vines wrapped and ripped, sending blood and bits of flesh flying in all directions as it pulled Captain Smith into itself.

The captain's face was twisted into an expression of both ecstasy and agony. He mewled and cried out, reveling in that pleasurable pain. One by one, the sacrificial hearts smoldered. Tiny lines of smoke wafted into the air as the hearts beat faster and faster. Theresa's chants grew even louder as the ritual reached its crescendo.

Then, as one, all of the hearts burst into flame, burning so hot and bright that Evelyn had to look away. As they burned, their original owners screamed into the night air.

The brightness died away, and Evelyn stole a glance. Standing by the fire was the Avatar of Sin. It dropped to all fours and walked closer to Evelyn. It still had the branchy antlers, but it was Captain Smith's bloody face instead of the elk skull.

"I am the doorway. I can see it now."

When he spoke, his voice creaked and groaned, like the breaking of branches and bone. The aspens around them whipped around in a frenzy; Evelyn saw they weren't trees at all but the appendages of something else. Something much bigger.

Evelyn looked for the Colt Navy. It was the only thing that could stop the Avatar now. However, she couldn't see it anywhere.

She tried to stand, and when she did, her hand grasped the handle of her hairpin dagger. Before she could get to her feet, a viny branch wrapped around her torso and dragged her closer to the Avatar. The blow to her head sapped most of her strength, leaving her with almost nothing left to fight back. Evelyn tried to twist away and stab at the vine, but the small dagger wasn't enough. The Avatar pulled her close, lifting her to eye level.

"The truth. I see it now," the Avatar said. "This world was never ours. We are specks of dust in the wake of the Root of a Thousand Eyes. The Root has seen the future, and only the faithful will be a part of it. When I open the door and awaken the Root, it shall crawl forth and cover this world with its many branches. Every living thing shall be a part of its glory... except you. You have been nothing but an annoying disease."

The Avatar's abdomen cracked open, forming into a maw with rows of wooden teeth. A ropy tongue that dripped a foul-smelling ichor whipped around expectantly. The inside of the creature's stomach was pitch black until a swirling void of cerulean light formed like a miniature galaxy.

"You will see with your own eyes now," the Avatar said.

All that strength and determination is in your eye. It's all in your eye.

As the Avatar moved her body closer to the open maw, Evelyn got an idea.

"I seek the truth," she said and stabbed the hairpin dagger into her own eye.

First, there was a sea of pain. Then there was nothing but darkness.

CHAPTER 16

The voice in the deep was all there was. The voice that guided Theresa's words, making her say those horrible incantations and sapping her very life-essence... the voice consumed her. Yet now it was gone.

Instead of its voice, Theresa could only hear the beat of her own heart. She opened her eye and winced as bright firelight blasted her senses. The world spun, and she fell onto the ground, staring up into the night sky.

The moon was full, and the stars were brighter than she had ever seen before. For eons, she stared at the sky, watching the stars move—watching the stars burn and fade away to nothing.

She could see it when the final star burned black, and the sky was nothing but a canvas of darkness. A giant doorway made of glowing purple energy. However, the door disappeared as Theresa snapped out of it.

All at once, the sound of crackling fire rushed into her ears. The sky changed again, but it was back to normal this time, covered with angry clouds. The taste of ash and soot coated the inside of her mouth, causing her to gag. Theresa hacked up a giant ball of black goo onto the grass. She stared at it for a moment and found tiny grey hairs. When she looked closer, she could see they were actually fine roots. Yet they started to move.

Theresa screamed and moved away as the roots whipped around in a frenzy before lying still. Her heart threatened to jump out of her throat, and Theresa wanted nothing more than to get up and run. However, something caught her attention.

Evelyn's voice.

Theresa turned around, and a little piece of her mind splintered with what she saw. A giant creature stood near a bonfire of purple flames holding Evelyn up with dozens of roots and branches that had split off its body and twisted into Evelyn's. Evelyn spoke words... *the words*... in a mind-less drone. Blood spilled from Evelyn's bloody eye-socket and ran down her cheeks while pitch-black smoke gushed from her skull.

The creature's torso had split open into some demonic mouth, and it lowered Evelyn's body into it.

Theresa tried to stand, but the world swayed, and she fell forward. Her hand brushed against something hard and cold, and an icy chill crawled up through her fingers, running up her arm. A voice slunk into her mind like a fox sneaking into a chicken coop.

You can kill it and end all of this. Just use me and send them to oblivion.

Theresa snatched her hand away and found Evelyn's Colt Navy lying in the grass. The plants had wilted all around the weapon, and using her true sight, Theresa could see wisps of red smoke wafting from the cylinder.

"Do it," Evelyn said.

Theresa looked up from the pistol to her friend. Evelyn was still in the throes of the ritual, about to locate the door, but Theresa also saw her friend's spirit standing nearby. She stood, bathed in white light, fading in and out of existence. Evelyn looked at her with her good eye and nodded.

"It's okay," Evelyn said.

"Please, don't make me."

Evelyn's spirit gave her a look that was full of love and care. She forced a smile.

"You have to, kid. There isn't another way."

"I can't," Theresa said. Tears ran down her cheeks. Her entire body shuddered as she sobbed.

"You can."

Evelyn's body pointed to the fire. The Avatar followed her gaze and laughed.

"The door! I can see it now!" the thing croaked.

The trees whipped and writhed all around them, and Theresa knew without a doubt that everything would come to an end if the door was opened. She had seen the truth.

It took all of her strength and grit to reach out and grab the pistol. The weapon's hate and rage poured into her, giving her the energy to stand and hold the weapon steady.

Yes. Now squeeze the trigger.

The moon disappeared behind a sea of black clouds. Rain began to fall from the sky as the angels above wept.

Theresa thought frantically, trying to figure out another way, but came up short. Especially as the creature lowered Evelyn's foot into its mouth.

"I'm so sorry," Theresa said. Tears welled in her eye and cut a path down her grimy, soot-stained cheek.

The gun barked louder than anything Theresa had ever heard. Time slowed down as the lead tore into Evelyn's chest, obliterating her heart and ripping the very soul from her body. It continued, blasting out Evelyn's back and slamming into the Avatar.

The trees screamed in pain and rage. In a matter of seconds, all the aspens in the immediate area withered, curling in on themselves like worms left out in the sun.

The Avatar dropped Evelyn to the ground before falling to its knees. Theresa aimed the pistol at the thing's head, feeling nothing but primal anger at Captain Smith. She was about to send another bullet into the monster when it fell to the ground, shriveling and crumbling to dust. The only thing left was the carved hand.

I'm so sorry.

Evelyn found herself lying on the ground next to the fire. It had long since burned out, leaving her cold. It was dark out, which made it difficult to see.

She rolled over onto her back and grimaced as her chest constricted. It felt like a heavy boot slowly applied more and more pressure to her torso, making it hard to breathe.

Evelyn sat up and looked around. None of the other people, dead or alive, were there.

"Theresa?"

There was no answer.

Evelyn got to her feet, but it took all of her energy to do so. The pain in her chest became heavier, and by the time she had taken two steps, she could hardly draw a breath.

"I... I can't...."

All around her, the darkness gathered. It swallowed the sky. It swallowed the fire's embers. It ate everything.

From the darkness came the sound of footsteps.

"Looks like I get to devour you, Evelyn Horn."

That voice. She had heard it many times before in her head. She had heard it that night long ago in that abandoned church that shouldn't have been. It was the Colt Navy.

The kid had done it.

Evelyn fell to the ground and laid her head onto the grass, ready to accept her fate. She was tired of fighting and welcomed oblivion.

However, before the darkness could touch her, a bright light formed behind her, full of warmth and love.

"No, this cannot be," the voice said.

The darkness swelled, but the light grew brighter, driving it back until it was gone.

"Beautiful star in heav'n so bright..."

It was Raymond's voice. But this time, Evelyn knew deep down, it was actually Raymond. Not some thing the darkness had sent to trick her.

Evelyn sat up, looking into the light. She could see the faint outline of someone standing in front of her.

"Raymond?"

"Hey there, Eve. It's time to go."

EPILOGUE

Theresa put the last bit of her supplies into Stinker's saddlebags. She stood outside of her tiny cabin and stared at it with a mix of sadness and anxious elation. Her time in the town of Ashley had been meaningful, but there was work to be done.

She pulled Evelyn's leather medicine bag with the snow-white raven feather and placed it around her neck. Some of the tension drained from her body, and a gust of wind tussled Theresa's hair.

"I'm going to miss you," Theresa said.

Stinker let out an anxious huff and nuzzled his nose into Theresa's shoulder. She patted the side of his cheek.

"It's okay, boy. You're with me now."

The Colt Navy sat in its place on Stinker's saddle. It still had two shots, and even though she would like nothing more than to throw it into a volcano and watch it melt away to nothing, the weapon could serve its purpose.

We could do great things, you and I. Just listen to what—

Theresa gripped the leather pouch around her neck and focused her will. The pistol's voice turned into a small buzz in the back of her head.

With that, Theresa mounted Stinker and rode away. Jackson Francis was still out there somewhere. Plus, Theresa knew if you wanted to kill a tree, you had to destroy the roots.

End

About the Author

C.R. Langille spent many a Saturday afternoon watching monster movies with their mother. It wasn't long before they started crafting nightmares to share with their readers. They are a retired, disabled veteran with a deep love for weird and creepy tales. This prompted them to form Timber Ghost Press in January of 2021. They are an affiliate member of the Horror Writer's Association, a member of the League of Utah Writers, and they received their MFA: Writing Popular Fiction from Seton Hill University.

If you enjoyed *Branches and Bone*, please consider leaving a review on Amazon or Goodreads. Reviews help the authors and the press.

If you go to www.timberghostpress.com you can sign up for our newsletter so you can stay up-to-date on all our upcoming titles, plus you'll get informed of new horror flash fiction and poetry featured on our site monthly.

Take care and thanks for reading *Branches and Bone!*

-Timber Ghost Press